WHERE GREEN
MEETS BLUE

CORINNE BEENFIELD

For John

Chapter One

Kentucky's Appalachian Mountains, May 1936

I never thought it would be hard to leave. People say it is, but to me, it seemed that it was the *waiting* that was most difficult, the trying to keep alive something precious buried so deep inside me. Staying was killing it off for sure, no matter how hard I tried to keep it beating.

At night, I would lie in bed and gingerly touch my swollen eyes, then trace my fingers along bruises hiding below my collar line. The heartache was particularly palpable on those nights, tender under my fingertips, and I could only wonder—when will the cage doors open? When will I take my luggage and walk down the gray paved road of my childhood for the last time? The waiting and wanting broke my heart. At times, they seemed the only things more excruciating than his fits of rage, but my planning had to be perfect. This I knew from too many imperfect attempts. So long as there was a scent to stalk Warren would follow the hunt.

When the moment came, though, there was no time

for executing plans. No bags were packed, no coins in my dress pocket. As I ran toward the back door, the box of things that had ignited his fury sat on the ground and I snatched the contents, knowing the consequences couldn't exceed what they already were.

The actual leaving was simple, simple as jumping on our mare and racing with blind direction, but I realize now it isn't easy. It doesn't breathe like I always thought freedom would, but instead my heart pounds so hard with fear, my mouth is filling with the taste of iron. Warren - for I never could call my father any term of endearment - had howled at my back as I took off, but it was when he fell silent that I started to shudder uncontrollably. That was when I knew he was turning his attention to the pursuit.

Terror tightens in my shoulders and locks my jaw as I ride, stiffening every muscle right down to the knuckles clutching the reins. It makes me so brittle, I could crumble to dust until I drift away into the cool night breeze. Is this the freedom I always waited for?

Even if I can somehow escape him, what do I do now? I don't have a penny to my name, a single change of clothes, not a speck of food for the journey ahead. Then there's the journey itself. As long as I can remember, I've had the decision made to leave, but where to go didn't matter. Not so long as it was *away*.

Now it matters.

These several miles, I've hardly even kept track of north until there is no way of knowing how close I may to be a town. If I can but find civilization, I might be able to beseech some kindness from strangers, but the only company I have here are the charcoal trees. Through their leaves, I look up to a star-soaked sky, and the sight of it makes me catch my breath and pull on the reins.

Lady stops, her breathing as heavy as my own. Tears

sting my eyes, and pure exhaustion causes me to stumble as I dismount. I catch myself on her neck and cling to her, my face buried in the soft brown mane. Dread has sapped me right down to the marrow of my bones and I find myself sinking to my knees, soft mud seeping through the long grass and onto the knees of my dress.

The treasured items have never left the crook of my arm but for the stolen ring which is pushed onto the end of my thumb. The other hand still shakes, the pain of the blisters there throbbing clear up my arm, white pus oozing where the reins have popped the sores. Bringing the treasures to my chest, I curve my back over them, though unsure if I am protecting them, or they me. They are my shield against the dark, the only shield I have ever known.

One by one, I touch the books.

It's too dark to read their titles, but I recognize them from the feel of their spines, their shape, the corners where they are scuffed up. I know them as well as if they were each a tangible piece of my soul, which in a way, I supposed they are. Or at least what I hope makes up my soul.

The Wonderful Wizard of Oz, its cover as green as wonder and dream dust, with loose pages falling from the binding and stuffed back in. Perhaps I never thought of where my journey would take me because it was always as distant and fantastic as Oz. Somewhere over the rainbow, over the mountains, into the next valley—that was enough for me. What a child I feel like, thinking of it now.

The Call of the Wild. The very touch of its dark cover seems to me what bravery would feel like if I could hold it in my hands. I cling to it, hoping it will spark that flint of courage in my heart, but the night feels as dark as ever.

And of course, *Don Quoxite,* the most loved and yet least battered, for we all protect what we love the very most.

The only tragedy of the three, but I am not so young as to believe that all roads are made up of glittering yellow brick, and not everyone *wants* to make it home. Yet it is my favorite all the same.

Last of all, the wedding ring. Tilting my head back to see it better, I hold it above my face with two fingers encircling the half moon above me. Such a tiny thing, where all this started. The best and worst thing to happen to me. For a split second, I am tempted to raise it above my head and throw it into the trees, letting the night swallow it whole. But I know I could never do that. With a slow exhale, I instead look down and slip it onto my right hand where it spins, slightly loose on my thin fingers.

Lady whinnies into the charcoal trees surrounding us, noticing before me a crunch of twigs under heavy weight. Every inch of me stiffens enough to shatter at the slightest touch, but I tell myself not to rise. Perhaps the unknown creature hasn't noticed us yet. Fresh sweat breaks across my skin as I imagine wolves and coyotes until my eyes can make out the silhouette of a man on horseback.

No. It can't be.

It's my father.

I would have preferred wolves.

How did his old horse travel this far? How did he know which direction I went? Maybe my father only sees Lady. Perhaps the tall grass hides me enough here. Crouching over onto my belly, I set the books down and try to make myself disappear, my fingers clawing into the dirt for rocks in case I must defend myself. It's a terrible plan. Every time I've fought back, things have ended worse for me. But I do it anyway. And this time I have more reason than ever—I can't give up my new freedom without the fight of my life. The fight *for* my life.

Behind me, I hear branches scathe his horse's sides,

then the scratch of a match being struck. I flinch as light bathes over me, knowing hiding just became impossible.

"Miss! Are you all right?"

My fingers let go of the rocks in my hands. I've never heard this voice before. I don't answer, but turn to face the stranger, grimy hand blocking the glare from my eyes. He holds the small fire so that he can more clearly see me, making it so I can hardly make out his features.

"What on earth are you doing out here?" he asks as his great silhouette reaches to the back of the horse and brings forth an unlit lantern. With a kiss from the match, it bursts to life, and I have to look away from the sudden contained star. Eyes falling on my dress, I see myself as he must be seeing me. Lying in the clearing has left dark stains of mud on me, and the wind from riding has torn my brown waves from their pins until they now fly wild about my face. Seizing the books next to me, I cling to them as if they were an infant he would try to pry from my arms.

"Aww," he answers his own question when I don't speak as he climbs down from his horse and offers a hand out to me. "You must be one of those book women I've heard about."

I have no idea what he is talking about, but I am not about to let him know that.

He waits, hand outstretched, as I sum him up. With thick dark curls and a clean jawline, he is the kind of handsome that stops most girls in their tracks—a strike against him, frankly. The Don Juans can always be trusted the least, I have found. They'll say anything, twist any truth just to get a girl to blush, or worse, to get her to act to their advantage.

He smiles, eyes shining with a charisma that he is probably used to having go straight to a girl's knees. I, however, just look at his extended hand, then lift myself from the ground. Rounding my shoulders as I stand, I hope mere bravado will keep him from thinking he can dare touch me. *I am the fairy queen Titania*, I recall from *A Midsummer's Night Dream*, my jaw set to meet his eyes. I nod slowly, as though he were a simple nymph of the forest. Everyone else my age has outgrown such imaginations, but I found long ago that they have a power to them. They keep me buoyant when everything else in this world would submerge me. I truly believe if it wasn't for these pretend-ings, everything I like most about myself would have been drowned years ago.

"You are awful far off track, aren't you?" He brushes his hand on his trousers, and I think I see a flush crawl up his neck. Looking away, I feel a gray guilt in my stomach. I hadn't meant to be unkind.

"My horse got spooked." I don't dare smile in case he takes it as an invitation, but I let my voice come out soft. "If you could direct me to town, I would be most grateful."

For a brief second, he looks at me, and I think he sees right through my white lie. But when his eyes lock on mine, I know my first assumption was incorrect. He smiles warmly, his gaze intent in a way I recognize, in a way that women never look at me.

Pinching my lips, I make my stare back cold. He shouldn't be looking at me like that. Even if he is a good man, it will only bring him trouble.

"There's a dry creek bed just over this way." He points east with a jerk of his head. "Follow it downhill and it will take you straight to Whitesburg. If you get your horse, I'll show you."

He begins making his way through the trees, leading his beautiful red-and-white horse on foot, before I can respond. As I reach for Lady's reins, she nuzzles my arm. "Come on, girl, just a bit farther," I urge her, rubbing her face with my free hand and praying I'm telling her the truth.

"I'm Henry Sterling," he calls over his shoulder, then pauses and looks back for me. "Am I going too fast?"

"Not at all." I pick up my pace and don't meet his eyes.

"That's better." He smiles. "It was hard to have a proper conversation when you were so far back. I felt a bit like a slave owner." He chuckles at his own joke, but his comment makes me feel like someone has stuck out their foot and tripped me. I've hardly said a handful of words to this man, and already he has struck too close to my secret. Making our footsteps match side by side, I tell myself never again to walk like someone owns me.

"I'm Marian," I respond with my real name out of habit, then catch myself before I let my last name slip.

"Marian...." He fishes for a last name. It feels too informal to only give the first, but I don't like lying more than I must.

"Do you live in Whitesburg?" I ask, hoping to derail him.

"No, my kids and I live in these mountains, so high we hardly see a soul. I was searching out a bobcat that's been lurking around our farm, but no luck yet. It's a wonder you book women come out to these parts unprotected. I wouldn't want it for my girl."

"Who says we are unprotected?" I raise an eyebrow in a bluff. The last thing I want to do is admit to a strange man in the darkness that I am completely defenseless.

But who are these book women he keeps speaking of?

"Well, good." He nods, his eyes on the lantern's glow. "You being sent up here is dangerous enough. It's wise to be prepared." He glances at me out of the corner of his eyes. "If I may ask, it seems a bit of an unusual occupation. Why do you do it?"

My mind flies in zigzags as I search for some answer. I had hoped that I wouldn't have to come up with a false story to feed him, but telling the truth is wildly out of the question. So I clutch to the only fragment of honesty I can share.

"I love books." I pause, hoping he'll pick up the conversation, but he just waits for me to go on. "More than anything else on earth, I love books."

He dips his head to the side, not quite a nod, no quite a shrug. "You'd have to. I've never seen anything like it. You ladies have more gumption than some mail carriers I've met. 'Neither snow nor rain nor heat' will stop the book women I've met. 'Nor gloom of night' either, apparently." He looks at me now and grins. It turns something in my stomach to gold, but light and free as sunlight. Swallowing, I grip Lady's reins tighter and throw my gaze to the trees ahead of us, but Henry stops suddenly.

"All right. This dry creek will see you home—you don't have even a mile to go." He hesitates. "Do you, uh, want me to see you down?" He scratches his neck and looks away.

"I'll be fine." I hope I assure him more than I have convinced myself.

He nods slowly. "I would, but my kids are waiting," He exhales, and I can see that he's torn. "My little girl, she worries. Hang on—take this." Reaching to his horse, he opens a satchel, and like pulling a rabbit from a top hat, he reveals a large mound wrapped in a thin cloth.

"Some bread. Where's your pack? It would be hard to ride well with your hands so full. Here, take mine—your books should fit too. There. Hurry on, now. I bet they are waiting up for you at the post office."

Post office? What has a post office to do with anything?

But I know better than to pull at the strings of the deception that has been woven.

"Thank you for your kindness," I answer. As the bread and the bag pass from his strong hands to mine, relief floods me over as if from an enchantment. I can make this stretch. This much bread can last a few days if I'm careful, and a few days may be enough for me to get on my feet. With food in my hands and my feet pointed in the right direction, suddenly the night doesn't seem so much black, as blank. Fresh. Waiting for a new day.

Perhaps I just might be okay.

Dropping the Queen Titania act, I meet Henry's eyes again. "You have no idea what this means to me." I find myself smiling at him for just a moment or two, and he doesn't hesitate to smile back. Dropping my gaze, I turn to Lady and heave myself onto her back.

Henry nods up at me from the ground and gently lays a hand on his own horse's neck. "Safe travels, Marian."

There is a purple tightening in my chest when he says my name, and I can only respond with a nod. Without another hesitation, I kick Lady's sides, my hands clenching tight on her reins.

I don't say goodbye. Farewells are for friends, and friends mean attachments. And "attachments," as far as I'm concerned, is just one more word for ropes that will bind and control you. I will be no one's puppet. Too much of my life has already been spent that way.

I dig my heels into my mare, and by moonlight, I try to make out the creek bed we must follow.

As I ride, the rush of wind immediately chills my skin and twines its fingers into my chestnut hair, making the waves brush against my shoulders and fly behind me. Over the creek bed, trees stretch and barely touch each other, as though passing a secret from one to the next. I strain my ears to hear their whispers through the leaves, but if they speak to me, I don't understand. But that's okay. Let them keep their secrets.

I have my own.

For the briefest moment, I dare close my eyes. Breathing in, I taste the *joy* of my new freedom for the first time, rich and sweet as pine mingled with magnolia. Opening my eyes, I lean my head back as though to howl at the moon, but instead, I breathe in the night, deep and soothing. Inhale. Exhale. Inhale. Exhale until something blue and beautiful fills me to the brim. The best feeling I know.

Hope.

Chapter Two

The town is made up of sunlight.

I awoke to it already high and hot, peering into the alley where I'd found warmth in the night against the outside of a bakery wall. I'd fallen asleep to the comforting sounds of early bakers, a reminder that I am not alone in the world.

Before emerging from the alley, I took plenty of time to run my fingers through my hair and pick dried mud off me, making myself as presentable as possible. I'll need to be presentable if I'm going to find a job.

After last night's conversation, a plan has formed in my mind. In one glance at my books and my horse, Henry had assumed me fit to be a book woman. I don't know what this means, but I intend to begin my search at the post office. Slinging the pack of books and bread over my shoulder, I rub my hand over Lady's smooth sides, the warm brown color of a fiddle.

"Don't look so concerned, sweetness. How about a little faith in me, huh?" I smile, hoping it will spark some bravery to chase away the fears of the day. Then placing a kiss on my fingers, I set it on her strong jaw as her dark eyes looked from me to the glare of the street, beckoning me as if to say, *"It's time to go out there. Time to face whatever the day may throw at us."*

Blowing out my air softly, I nod, and tug on her reins.

Stepping from the alley, my eyes pinch in protest to the light, but I grin. It's beautiful.

Heaven might have streets of gold, but this entire town is covered in it. Amber sunlight is everywhere, glowing off the yellow brick buildings, reflecting from the windows, even hanging in the dust. Sunlight, apparently, smells like slightly overripe fruit, the kind perfect for the picking that shouldn't be left for any other day. It's meant to be enjoyed *now*.

Both cars and horses pepper the street in front of me. Even a few carriages are being pulled. A Hoover carriage approaches me, and I would chuckle if it wasn't a sign that this economic depression has hit its owners particularly hard. With its engine taken out, a broken-down car is a reasonable weight for a horse to pull, and as it passes me, a little boy rests his face against the car's window. We lock eyes. Lifting my hand, I give him a little wave, but he doesn't smile back.

Turning my gaze to the rest of the townsfolk, I see the same heaviness in their features. People bustle through the winding streets, sweat on their foreheads and a shuffle in their steps. I realize that they only see bleached buildings and dry, baked-down roads. They don't even realize they live in El Dorado.

"The natives have no idea what they are sitting upon," I whisper to Lady so no passerby will think I'm mad. I quietly try out my best Spanish accent, and just like that, the day's struggle becomes an adventure, a challenge of the best sort. "Many men have died trying to find El

Dorado, yet here we stand." I smile. "Perhaps if the natives take a liking to us, they will think I'm a goddess." Shrugging, I drop the accent and give a playful glance at Lady. "Though I'd be happy just for a job."

I mount Lady and we take to the streets at a trot. I try to sit tall in the saddle as though I have boatloads of men backing me up, as though I am a conquistador and don't even know what fear is.

It takes no more than five minutes to trot down the main street when I see a sign reading "United States Postal Service" directly above the door of a simple, square white-plank building. However, it's another board, brand new and out of place as it's mounted to the side, that quickens my heart to a gallop. "WPA Packhorse Library." Something silver courses through my veins at those words.

Sliding off Lady, I find a rail to tie her to. "*That* is where our fortunes lay. If I go there, we may become rich beyond our wildest dreams. *Or,*" I pause for dramatic effect. "They may offer me as a gift to the volcano god." Giving her an exaggerated gulp, I wish for a moment I could stay with Lady and not have to face whatever unknown will be on the other side of those doors. But it's time to behave like an adult again, and from El Dorado, the only gold I can take with me is my courage.

Stepping through the front door, I hear voices.

"It's a *cliff edge*. Who would live up there? They clearly don't care for visitors to build their home in such a forsaken place, and I won't risk my life to get there." A woman stands, arms folded, on one side of a desk crammed into a corner. A thin, graying man sits on the other, and in between them lays a mound of books, each cover a different color like the jewels they are. "A person would have to be crazy to travel it just to take a pile of books to people who can barely even read."

A smile tugs on the corner of my lips. *I* am just that sort of crazy. Turning toward the desk, I stand behind the woman as she rants on.

"I don't care how tough times are. Twenty-eight dollars a month is not worth losing my life. I'm sorry, Alvin. My mind is made up."

"It wasn't two months ago that you stood here, begging me for this job." The man's skin looks as dry and thin as paper, crinkling at his edges. "Telling me your children would starve if you couldn't find work. Have you forgotten already?"

Leaning forward, she pushes the mound of books toward him as her voice lowers. "If I die, they will starve only faster. I'm *done*."

She stalks away, leaving the books. For all the wear of their covers, they still sparkle, calling to me as treasure does to a pirate.

"I would like her job." I step forward. At the door, she catches my words and stops in her tracks, but doesn't bring herself to look at me. The man she had called Alvin snags her eye, and he can't hide his pinched smile. With a snort through her nose, she pushes through the door and is gone.

"So." Alvin turns his attention to me. "You would like a position as a packhorse librarian?"

"If that's what her job was, then yes, I will take it." I nod, planting my feet like Julius Caesar.

To that, he just leans back and looks me over, running his fingers along the gray stubble on his cheek, his eyes squinting as though he can't see me clearly. "You don't know what the job entails?"

For a moment, doubt fills my belly, yellow and rotting. I hear the words in my head that were whispered to me ever since I was a child, whenever the drink would loosen Warren's tongue. *You think you are somebody? You think anyone on this planet cares about you? You only have* me. *Without me, you are nothing, a nobody.*

There hasn't been a day I haven't had to tell myself he's wrong. Even when it seemed like he was right, I told myself he was wrong. If I was only lying to myself, at least it was a good lie. A lie worth believing.

Rolling my shoulders back, I answer Alvin across the desk. "I have a horse, a passion for books, and I know how to feel fear without letting it stop me. If there are other requirements, I shall find a way to fulfill them."

He stops rubbing his papery cheek, and for a moment just meets my eyes. Then he nods, and a soft smiles stretches across his face.

"It's part of Roosevelt's New Deal," he explains, then motions to a window with a view of the mountains. "This Depression has hit no one harder than our Kentucky mountaineers. They have nothing, and no way to better their circumstances. Many have never even stepped foot in a school. Yet they see that if there is any way out of poverty for their children, it is through *these*." He waves his hands over the books, proud as a new father. The image sticks in my mind, and I wonder if this is a man who sees books for what they are. Who understands that if there is magic on this earth, it is in these small bound pages. "They are hungry for books, but they can't leave their fields and cattle. So the packhorse librarians are going *to them*." A glint catches in his eye, and I can tell he's honored to be part of this. "The New Deal grants us no funds for books, so we must run on donations. Most are castaways from old schools, and many households gave what few they had. We have no library to operate from, so Pack Horse Libraries across Kentucky are taking up headquarters in court-houses, churches, or . . ." He pauses and waves about him.

"Post offices," I finish his sentence.

He points at me with a grin as though to say, *exactly*.

"Your routes will cover about one hundred and twenty miles per week," he continues. "Each day for a week will be a different route, then you will repeat the cycle, dropping off new books for the people to read and retrieving old ones. You will find that they will be expecting you exactly a week from the day that they saw you last." I like the way he says, "you will." as though the job is already mine.

But it is not simple enough to get the job. In this economy, asking for a job and being granted it on the spot is a blessing unheard of, but I must ask more if I am to survive.

"Sir," I lower my eyes for the first time since arriving, "I must be frank with you. There is nothing I would like more than to take this position. However, at this time I have nowhere to live." I swallow, hating the red, audacious words before they even come out. "If I could have an advance, I could find a roof to put over my head. I give you my word, I will be your most dedicated employee. I will cover more routes, go a farther distance, whatever is needed. Weather cannot deter me." I think of Henry's comment last night. "I would take my job more seriously than a mail carrier does. Yet to do it, I must have some shelter." I have kept my gaze down as I spoke, but when he doesn't answer right away, I have to bring myself to look up at him.

"Tell me this." His voice is quiet, and I realize how shockingly blue his eyes are. "Are you running *from* trouble, or are you *bringing* trouble?"

It's a heartbeat before the word comes out. "From." My eyes dart to the door, as if Warren will walk through it any moment. "But I cannot guarantee that it will not follow me."

Alvin nods twice before speaking. "I cannot give you an

advance, but I have a small barn. My wife has made more quilts than we know what to do with, and we could make the loft quite comfortable for you to sleep in. It isn't much, but it would be shelter from animals during the summer, and you'd be welcome to use the house for washing up and to care for yourself. It would give you a few months to save up before fall comes and the barn is too cold to sleep in. Some would say it's not fit for a lady, but then, sleeping on the streets doesn't exactly have much decorum. Will it suffice?"

I don't hesitate. "Oh, yes, thank you!" I close my eyes to keep them from tearing, and turn my face away. "I am a stranger to you, yet you'd trust me——" I choke on the last word and don't say another.

As I open my eyes, he smiles at me, his wrinkles in all the right places. Turning his attention to the books on the desk, he lifts the cover from the top book and pulls out a map that was tucked inside it. "These are the routes she just left. They are yours now." When he hands me the map, I see that its creases are already worn colorless, and water has contorted the top of it. It is hope, folded up and ready to carry in my pack. Taking it in my fingers, I feel something blue and sweet swell in my chest as he reaches down and lifts the treasures off the desk, offering them to me. "Can you start today?"

Chapter Three

Tree leaves drip from last night's rain as I walk by Lady's side, with each step her feet sinking into the mud. Four days in, four routes in, and I've gotten us lost exactly four times now. "It will be fine," I assure Lady as she whinnies in argument. "Remember . . ." I stroke her face, trying not to let her hear the discouragement in my voice. Hunger makes me breathless, and each word takes effort I probably shouldn't be wasting. "The *plan* is to get lost. So everything is going according to plan." Giving the reins a yank, I shiver from the cool raindrops soaking through my thin dress. I try to call my mind back to the *good* moments of the last few days. Of children running when they saw my horse coming, of two teenagers acting out a favorite scene in *Robinson Crusoe*. And at the end of each day, Alvin's sweet wife Elleny would be waiting with some small snack, a peach or some grilled zucchini, and conversation on the porch.

"I wish we could offer you more food," Alvin had said that first night. "But we are almost out of last year's stock, and somehow we have to make it last until the harvest.

With running the WPA Library, I haven't been able to go hunting for meat. I can, however, teach you what berries of the mountains are safe to eat." He showed me how to distinguish elderberries from their poisonous imposters, where best to find ground cherries, and I already knew what wild watercress looks like. Between that and Henry's bread, I have barely kept from starving, though I always feel as if the insides of my stomach are rubbing together.

But the bread is nearly gone, and with each bite that becomes smaller it seems to be dwindling hope. I had always known when I dreamed of running away that it would be difficult to survive. That I would go hungry, that I would have to find a means of providing for myself. Even when I took this job, I knew it would be unlike anything I had ever done before. But to ride a horse down trails marked "Cut Shin Pass" or "Troublesome Way"? What was I *thinking?*

There is a difference, I am learning, between knowing and knowing. Knowing *about* something, and knowing from *experience*. I had heard the woman in the post office fume about the struggle of the job, of fearing for her life, but it did nothing to deter me. That was until yesterday, when Lady balanced on a cliff edge, the home I was traveling to a speck on the mountainside, and with each step of my mare, I clenched her tighter with my thighs, both of our breaths short and jagged. When I handed the family the load of library books—my most precious three safely in Alvin's barn—for the first time, they seemed *just books*. For the first time, I wondered if they were worth the price being asked of me.

Shaking my head to dispel the petrifying memory, I come back to this moment. It's not a wild improvement. I'm up to my ankles in mud and up to my neck in despair. I try to rally courage for Lady, as though she is my child watching for my reaction in order to know how to feel herself. "The worst days are over," I whisper, but no more comes out. Right now I can't lie, even if it's just to myself and my horse.

There is no ignoring my options.

I could go back.

I would be beat within an inch of my life, but I know my father wouldn't finish me off. It would take me days to recover, feeding myself soft foods with swollen fingers. And he would feel ever justified as he ate from his own plate of ego and victory. How could I even think of going back?

But then, how can I not? I never knew true hunger. How quickly you assume you know how you'd feel in someone else's shoes. I couldn't have known the terror of slow starvation, the way it feels to have your insides want to eat themselves alive. Either I go back and live a half life, a cursed life, or I stay here and slowly die, fed only on the deteriorating belief that they there might be better days. There is no promise that those better days will ever come, and this is simply one of those mornings when I am finding it particularly hard to hope.

Up ahead, through the trees I make out logs linked together like a child's stacking toy. "Lady, a fence!" I grab at the mare's long face to show her, then lead the way. "We'll follow it! Sooner or later, it's bound to meet up with a road or bring us to a farm or *something*." I try to move quickly, but hunger slows me, leaving me out of breath. But soon, we come to the fence, and I collapse upon it as I gather air back into my lungs. Lady nuzzles my arm, soaking the sleeve with her wet fur, but I manage a smile. On the other side of the fence, large fields are cleared of trees, and wheat is thick and lush as a lion's mane. The fields rise and fall over a hill, and at the far end sits a cabin like a watchtower over the land.

Unfolding my map, I prop it over the logs of the fence and compare the drawings of blue and black against the landscape. Before taking this job, my experience with maps was limited to those drawn in the front of fantasy novels, and I've never even held a compass. But tracing my finger along one black threading line, I tap the tiny square at the end. "I think that's where we are supposed to be taking today's books," I tell Lady as I fold up the map. "Best not cut through the field, though, in case the witch uses her poppy magic to make us fall asleep," I borrow from *The Wonderful Wizard of Oz*. "It certainly wouldn't take much. A single poppy could do it." The words fall heavy around me like stones, no magic touching the field and turning it to red flowers. But it's when it's hardest to imagine that I need it the most.

I give Lady a weak smile, and her beautiful brown eyes linger with mine. It's not nearly as muddy here, and I heave myself onto Lady's back, grateful to give my shaking legs some rest. "Well . . ." I lean into her mane and stroke her neck. "The wizard is waiting. Let's go."

Lady covers the distance before long, and I look up with weary eyes to the tiny cabin along the horizon line where green fields meet blue sky, a barn tucked back behind it. "The Emerald City is even more beautiful than I dreamed," I whisper to Lady, giving her a nudge forward with my heels.

As we approach my gaze falls on a boy I hadn't noticed before, but he had clearly spotted me. His walk is determined and fast, yet not at all the buoyant steps of the other children who have greeted us on the other routes. He waves his arms as if to shoo us off, and my forehead furrows in confusion.

"I told you," he hollers, "not to bother coming here again. We don't need to be wastin' our time on your chicken scratch." The boy can't be older than ten, but from the commanding tone of his voice, it's plain he thinks himself a man.

Sitting tall in my saddle, I meet his eyes and he stops, folding his arms.

"Oh. What happened to the other Book Woman?" He squints up at me, mouth pinched thin as a pencil, no attempt to hide that he already doesn't like me. It will take some work to loosen the pole out of his trousers.

"I dropped a house on her," I answer straight-faced before climbing down. "You don't need to worry about her anymore. The Wicked Witch of the East is gone for good."

Face-to-face with the boy, I see his details. He has dirty blond hair, the tips lightened by the sun, though the sun has played a different number on his skin. A deep tan covers him that can only come from working hard or playing hard. His pants are about two seasons too small, showing ankles as thin as antlers and calloused bare feet. I've always had an odd respect for those who go bare-footed. Tipping my head, I give him a grin.

He doesn't smile back.

"Well, she should have told ya not to bother haulin' *those*," He points to my pack tied to Lady, lip curling as though the load smells. "A hard morning's ride for nothin'. You go on and get now. I got cows to get back to."

His words echo inside me as though trapped in a tin cage, my mind refusing to process them. They don't even *want* these books? No, I didn't go through all this for *nothing*...

"Wait!" a young voice calls out as the cabin door swings open and a girl dressed in soft blue like skydust flies out. She throws herself between me and her brother, grab-bing my wrists with hands covered in dough. "He was out of turn sending you away last time! I thought you'd never come back, but you're here!" She beams, dark curls feathering her face, with a smile she surely stole from the angels.

"Ah." I turn to Lady and untie the pack. "A flying monkey tried to scare me and Toto off." I gesture to Lady with a grin, and avoid looking to see what the boy thinks of being referred to as a winged chimpanzee. "But we couldn't give up. These are for you, my dear." Pulling the books from my bag, I bestow them upon the young girl. She gives a triumphant grin to her brother and pulls them to her. There in the matted grass, she sits and opens the first one. My heart leaps for the adventure she is about to have, remembering the feeling each book contains, like stepping into Oz.

Until I realize she has the book upside down.

I crouch down next to her and try to turn the book, but she holds tightly to it.

"Don't you know how to read?" I ask.

She looks at me, on her level, then shakes her head. "No, but if you bring me old school books, I learn fast. I learned how to whistle with no one teaching me, and I'm old enough to go to school if it wasn't so far."

Our eyes lock, and I feel something between the young girl and myself, like one heartbeat or a collective pulse. We both grip the book, and suddenly I realize I *need* this. Not the book itself—I need more than to hand off my loads to strangers. I have to feel like it *means* something to them. I have to share it with them.

"Could I teach you?" I ask without smiling because it's not an offer—it's a plea. It' as if my world spins on the answer of this young girl. If she says no what is to keep me from returning to my half life? My hunger alone could drive me there. But to have something bigger than myself, something to hope for, to work for—*that* is worth crossing mountains.

"Would you?" She jumps to her feet and hops about like a finch, gold and bringing joy in the gray mundane of my winter.

She clings to my fingers and jumps up and down, as I laugh and nod in response. "I'm Marian."

"Ah, if it isn't that Book Woman." I hear a familiar voice behind me, and the hairs on my arms rise.

Spinning around, I see Henry, his beautiful red-and-white horse trotting next to him. For a moment, my world stops breathing, as if all of nature is waiting to see how I will answer him. Of course, I'm very aware of how his kindness has kept me alive this past week. This is no small thing, and I do not treat it lightly.

Yet.

If I show my gratitude, it could be a spark of possibility, a beginning between us. I see it in his eyes, I feel it in the quickening of my pulse, and I cannot let that happen. To care for another person is to give them permission to hurt you, to make yourself vulnerable, to lie at their feet waiting to be kicked. In every face I see it—how we all go through life love-starved, not one of us getting all the love we want. Best to accept it, to find love for yourself and things that have no power to inflict pain back at you. I have known what it was like to pray that a gentle glance would fall on you, to cling to any tiny symbol that someone might care. My childhood was spent wanting nothing more than to be loved in return, and after all that time, I only found myself bleeding to death.

So I retreated. Long before I ran away, I built the loveliest walls around me, a castle to protect what is beautiful in this world from the evils that would try to assault it. A castle made of imagination and filled to the brim with my books. It was the only time I had known peace. With my bricks and my books, I curled my back against the heartache. That castle became home, and though I am far from where I was raised, I carry it with me. In these walls I stay, the only safety I know.

And it's obvious looking at Henry's dark eyes, the shade of a storm over a forest, that my heart would not be safe if those walls were to crumble.

The world exhales, and he speaks again. "I see you met Rosalie and Jesse." He gestures to the children.

"She's going to teach me to read!" Rosalie has not stopped leaping about, and she runs to her dad and pulls on his arms. "And then I'm going to teach *you!*" She giggles at the thought and Henry flushes, looking away.

"I *told* her we're too busy." Jesse looks at his sister as if something has begun to deteriorate. "When would they do their lessons? We don't need Rosalie sittin' still as a stone over that chicken scratch when there's work to be done."

"I'll still get all my chores done, I promise! Say she can come!" Rosalie drops to the matted ground again, gathering the books in her arms, and holding them to her heart in a way I have done a million times.

"I'm sorry." Henry's shoulders slump as he talks to his daughter on the ground. "Jesse is right—I don't see when we would have any time to spare. If we are going to keep this farm afloat, I need your help. I know it's a lot to ask of a girl your age, but if we don't do all we can—"

"The lessons themselves wouldn't take much time." I look away from the group, over Lady's back, hoping they won't see the desperation in my eyes. I'm uncomfortable with the idea of spending extra time on Henry's land, but this isn't about Henry. Not only do I need this, but his daughter should have this chance. What child, no older than seven, can spend sunup to sundown working hard labor on a farm? Where is the childhood without some imagination? Without it, they become grown too fast, like this Jesse before me. Her father cannot deprive her of this! "I could only teach her once a week when my route brings me this way. There are other mountaineers I have to take books to on the other days."

"We couldn't pay you for your time." He shakes his head and dismisses the idea with a wave of his hand. "Thank ya mighty anyways."

"Oh." I flush, embarrassed. "I'm not trying to make money off you. The lessons would be free as air. And I wouldn't have to distract her from her work. I could join her, help her get the work done faster so she has time to study and read."

Henry tips his head to look at me, his eyes soft. "That's an awful lot of work at the end of your long day. I bet you'd be right ready to be heading home."

How much do I have to twist this man's arm to get him to accept pure gold into his home? Before he can finish his sentence, I'm shaking my head, "No, really, there's no other way I'd rather spend my time. I'd *love* to teach her to read." They *can't* turn me away. I'm inclined to go against his wishes and come anyway, teach her in secret if I must, but after what he did for me, how could I? If he would but allow the girl these lessons, *this* would become the reason I could keep waking up each morning. This could keep me from going back to my father. "Please." I look at Rosalie as I speak, my thumb fiddling nervously with the stolen wedding ring on my hand. "Every soul alive needs some purpose."

It's quiet, and I can't bring myself to look at Rosalie's expectant face, or see Henry's dismissal. So instead, my eyes fall on Jesse. He locks his gaze with mine for just a moment, and in that split second, he seems exactly ten, not the man he makes himself out to be.

"Here's an idea." Henry's voice breaks into my

thoughts, his voice softer than before. "We come in from the fields each day to eat lunch—that's our big meal of the day. Marian, I'm pretty sure you intend to eat lunch as well, so you might as well eat it here. Every Tuesday, we will make a little extra, and when you bring the books, you and Rosalie can study and eat on the porch. Will that do? Rosalie, you can use mealtimes to practice your words."

Rosalie throws her arms about her father and I laugh at the girl, not meeting Henry's eyes, not daring to let him see how he has saved my life once again.

Chapter Four

❧

I see the small family before they see me. The ground smolders in the heat of the afternoon, leaving a haze between us. The cicadas sing their soulful harmony so loudly that the three of them don't hear my horse coming up the trail at all. Rosalie carries a metal bucket nearly as high as her waist, limping along under the weight as if she has a peg leg. Her face is shaded by a white hat so large, it clearly must be her father's. As I watch, she comes to the pigpen and carefully tips the canister onto its side until it rests against the bottom log of the fence. Then she pushes from the bottom and it all tips in to a trough as she calls, "Sue-ee!" And the hogs come running.

In the field Jesse grips a large plow, which dwarves him. Henry is securing the plow lines onto his horse's yoke, and from how he motions with his arms, I can tell he's giving directions to the young boy. Henry's skin is tanned from the hours spent on the farm, and the sweat makes him look made of polished stone. As he speaks, Jesse's eyes are wide, and his hands clutch the plow as if it might burst into flames if he didn't. I would chuckle at his intensity, but something about the moment infuriates me. How can Henry expect so much of his children? How can he rob them of their childhood?

"Avast, ye buccaneers!" I call out, pulling the pack of books from behind me. I lift it high above my head as though freshly pillaged. "I brought treasure, I have! All hands on deck to see the booty!"

Henry looks up at me and smiles, holding a hand to block the sun from his eyes as he straightens. My heart flickers and my mouth goes dry. I pinch it flat as a plank and look to the children instead.

Jesse seems to be finishing an extravagant eye roll, and he cracks the reins so the horse will plow forward and away from us. How can someone so young be so bitter?

"That's it! Ha! Well done!" Henry calls after him.

"You came!" Rosalie cries, dropping the empty bucket and running to Lady as I dismount. Her blue eyes catch the sunlight as she runs. The same shade as her brother's, but where his make me think of ice, hers make me think of a warmed shallow pool. "We made extra for lunch, but Jesse said you wouldn't come and that it would be a waste."

"That scallywag." I squint as though wearing an eye patch. "For that, we be keeping our treasure to ourselves, aye?"

She giggles, and as she cranes her neck back to look at me, she has to grab the large hat from tipping off her head. Slipping her hand in mine, she pulls me forward. "I set up lunch for us on the porch. Come on. Dad, she's here! We can eat now!" She stretches out an arm to her father.

He strides toward us, his dark curls matted against his forehead from the heat.

"Yes." I motion to Jesse in the field. "Let the boy have a break as well. I can teach all of you during lunch."

"He already ate." Henry rests a hand on the cabin porch railing. "He's anxious to get this field plowed before it gets too hot."

"Seems a big job for a boy so young." I don't look at him as I open up my bag of books and pull them out, setting them on the table Rosalie has led me to. The words come out barbed, and I regret them as I look at the table set with bread and butter, apple chunks and cheese. Even grape juice. Knowing the families I bring books to, this is likely a more extravagant meal than they can afford. Even the pack in my hand—Henry's old pack—criticizes me for being too abrupt. But I know what it's like, to have a childhood robbed from you. To be asked—no, *demanded*—to grow up too soon. How could I *not* cling to books, the only tether that still links me to that great ship of dreams and fairy dust?

My desperation to teach these children to read has grown, I realize, beyond even giving a purpose to my life. They *deserve* to have a childhood, and no matter how adamantly that is being stripped away from them, if I can but infuse these precious pages into their lives, perhaps these years of awe and magic won't be lost from them.

"He's capable," Henry answers, his smile only slightly fading. "Have a seat." He pulls a chair out for me, as though we weren't a couple of impoverished strangers trying to survive in the mountains, but distinguished aristocrats at a fine banquet. "What will you be starting your lessons with?"

"Thank you for your generosity. It looks delicious." I may be curt, but no one can say I don't have manners. "The twenty-six letters of the alphabet, and each has a sound."

Henry leans back, for once holding himself less like a captain and more like a cabin boy. His sudden vulnerability surprises me, and I feel an impulse to reach out, touch his strong hand, reassure him that it's okay not to know something so long as one is willing to learn. But I only pick up a piece of bread and butter it without looking at those dark, deep eyes that I can feel resting on my face.

"Really, before I begin, I think it would be wise to fetch the boy. He needs this." I pause. "Whether you realize it or not." I know there is an accusing tone in my words, but I don't care. I'm right. My gaze falls on the child, alone in the field, his thin arms struggling to control the large plow.

"Miss Marian." Henry's eyes fix on his boy as well, then he looks straight at me. "I may not be able to read, but I am not stupid. If there is anything I want for my children, it's for them to better their circumstances. Reading can do that—I know this. But . . ." He leans forward. "It's not the *only* way. I am raising them to be hard working and not because I like the sound of my own voice barking orders. Hard work shows them that if they will just put their shoulder to the wheel and be patient, they can achieve great things. They have greatness in them, and it starts on this farm, *but will not end here.*" He swallows once, his face serious. "*That* is my goal. If you can help with that, you are welcome at our table and we're grateful for your time."

I flush and look down, fiddling with the wedding ring on my hand. Rightly so, it doesn't feel like it belongs there, spinning on a finger that is just slightly too small. Touching it, I see Warren's rage when he caught me with it, light brown hair that is normally carefully combed back falling over his eyes as he slammed the door and came for me with his fists. Over those years, I had known those fists many times. Each hit aged me, for while the body ages with the passing of days, the soul ages with experience. Bit by bit, my father took my childhood from me. How I would have rather remained young in body and soul.

"Perhaps," I swallow and force each word out. "I have been seeing the world not as it is, but as I am." I pause and meet Henry's eyes, his arm protectively across the back of Rosalie's chair. His thumb bumps against her shoulder and she is relaxed at the touch, no tightening in her jaw, no plea in her eyes. As the touch of a father should be. My gaze lowers to my plate. "Please don't send me away."

It's quiet a moment while I wait for Henry's verdict.

"And have ye take the treasure chest with ye?" He answers in the worst pirate accent I ever heard. I look up at him and find myself smiling at him. "I should be thinkin' not. I'd walk the plank first, I would." He stands and Rosalie's eyes sparkle, looking up at him. Reaching down, he tosses her ringlets, a perfect but longer match to his own dark curls.

And here I sit, behind my walls, peeking over the turrets to a land I have never set foot in. They live in a different world from me.

"Well, there are decks to swap and rigging to repair. I best be going." He smiles again. "You two better get digging." He taps the top book in my stack with a finger and raises an intrigued eyebrow at Rosalie. "Rumor is, there's gold in there."

Looking in my eyes, he smiles at me and I can't help but smile back. It lasts longer than most smiles, no need for words commandeering our mouths. Then with a slow nod, he turns and steps off the porch. I watch his footfalls, steady and constant as the waves, and suddenly notice how I'm not the only one watching him. Rosalie crawls into my lap, but doesn't take her eyes from her father, and Jesse looks up from the fields as though sensing Henry's presence near. They look at him like one would a compass, like it will tell them which way to go to make it through a starless night. Like they trust him completely. I don't think I've ever looked at anyone in the world like that.

A silver something pumps from my heart and down my arms, leaving tiny goosebumps on my skin.

At first glance, I knew he was handsome. But something in how his arm was slung on Rosalie's chair, in the intensity of his eyes when he spoke of his children, of the playfulness in his terrible pirate accent makes me look at him differently. Suddenly I see. He's beautiful.

My eyes drop to my hands and the ring glares back up at me, accusing. *Keep your heart safe in your rib cage. It cannot be.* I know it can't. I'm not fool enough to believe that I have disappeared down a rabbit hole into another world where no one can reach me. At any moment, Warren could step back into my life, teeth grinding and fists clenched. I can't put Henry in that danger. Any of them.

But even if my father never found me, I know better than to let myself love. For a moment in Henry's smile, I saw it glisten at me, but it's only fool's gold in my pan. Perhaps there are those who strike it rich, but I am not one of them. The search will only leave me drenched and destitute. Better to put my heart into a life I *can* obtain.

Reaching forward, I trace an *X* across the top book. "Well, every pirate knows that under an *X* is where the treasure waits," I speak out loud to the tiny girl. "Let's begin."

How I wish I could share it with *all* of them.

In my mind, I can imagine us around the one table, Rosalie on my lap as Jesse rests his head in his palms, elbows on the table. And Henry to my side, his soft gaze on my face and hand in my own, as with the other I prop up *Don Quixote* and read aloud.

But some things cannot be. Somethings are safer not to imagine.

Chapter Five

E ach house on the street where Alvin and Elleny
live looks like it has a story inside it. Though the
street is fairly quiet now, there are still swings that
sway along with the branches of old willows. Pieced-
together birdhouses on poles stick into the flowerbeds,
painted all the more beautifully for the small unskilled
hands that did the job. Even though the builders of the
tiny perches have long moved away, the swallows and
yellow warblers still call this place home, and I think wait
to welcome the now-grown children when they come for a
visit to their aging parents. These are the sort of homes I'd
always imagined, the sort you want to return to and
still can.

I loved this street the first time I set foot on it. These
houses almost seem to breathe, almost seem human, they
have such personality. And the moment Alvin welcomed
me in for the first time and I crossed the threshold, I knew
that though this house is still, it is far from empty. It is filled
right up to the brim with memories—it is alive with them.

I wonder if their children can still feel the heartbeat of this place even if they are thousands of miles away.

Technically, only one is thousands of miles away—their youngest daughter who married a man intent on home-steading the last frontier, Alaska. The other two daughters married and live close enough that Alvin and Elleny see them about monthly, they say, and there is a bachelor son who is pursuing an education in another state but apparently makes it home for the holidays. Sometimes I try to imagine their moments growing up here. A small girl, asleep on the sofa and a younger Elleny collecting her daughter to put to bed. Or Alvin and his boy, one grown and the other young, leaning over the black-and-cream chessboard that still sits out. I can nearly see them, Alvin deciding whether or not or just how much to let the boy win.

I look at it now as I rub my wet hair with a soft towel. As powerful as my imagination is, I can't even picture my father calling a place like this home. The comparison is stark—where this living room has mismatched furniture and piles of books that have wandered from their shelves, the house I had grown up in had fine furniture strategically placed to cover holes where the walls had been punched in. The walls were the victims on the days Warren showed restraint. I wonder if those walking on our street ever guessed at the story our house told or if they just dropped their gaze, preferring not to know.

"How's it fit?" Elleny steps into the room, and her eyes scan the dress she gave me to change into after bathing. "Like a dream!" She is carrying the tray of water from the ice box and quickly she returns her gaze to it in order to make sure it doesn't spill. Then her voice lowers as she grumbles to herself. "Soon as we hit better times, I'm getting me one of those lovely refrigerators, and never have

to do this again. Get the door for me, will you, honey?"
Her eyes dart one more time to admire the dress on me,
and satisfied, she gives a nod. "That color looks beautiful
on you." Her thoughts ping-pong, always seventeen things
on her mind at once.

"You sure she wouldn't mind?" I smooth the worn blue
cotton over my hips, then step toward the door and
open it.

"If she left them, she doesn't want them," Elleny says
as she dumps the water on purple sage growing by the
front steps. Lines gentle as spider webs crease her face, but
her hair remains a pale blonde and flows about her shoulders. Her shape is soft as someone who has known child-
birth and years of knowing she's loved just as she is. It's her
quickness that surprises you. She moves as if never to let
old age catch her, and when she speaks, one can hear the
echo of younger years in her voice. "She says Alaska is no
place for skirts, and has taken up those awful men's
britches some of our own packhorse librarians have started
wearing." Elleny looks to me to agree with her, but I just
smile down at the open chest of dresses. To me, britches
make perfect sense for the job, but I'm not about to argue
the disadvantages of skirts when I only have one to my
name and she has offered four of her daughter's old ones.
These past three weeks, Elleny has let me wear some of
hers, though they have not fit well and are clearly for an
older woman. Each day, she insisted she just *knew* one of
her daughters had left some dresses behind, and at last it
was unearthed in the attic. "Have you tried the brown one
yet? Just take the whole trunk in the bathroom, we want to
see each one." she lifts the dark dress as she speaks. "It's
out of style. I passed it onto the girls from when I was
younger. My father bought it for me when I moved out.
Long as I live, I'll remember the train station, him trying

not to cry. Such a man. But you'll never find a dress of better quality. Made to last, you see?"

"This is so good of you. Thank you." I smile as Alvin enters the room, and when our eyes meet, he smiles. Though I've only been staying in the loft of their small, tidy barn less than a month, there is a feeling of being a flower pressed in a book—that they are shaping me, helping me hold on to what is good and beautiful. And, I like to think, maybe I'm imprinting on their story as well.

"Aww now, *this one* you should wear the next time you go to the Sterling farm." She pulls out a flowing dress of peony color and holds it to my shoulder bones. The color drains from my face and I frantically look at Alvin, who raises his frail hands as he sits in an armchair as if to say, *Don't look at me.*

"Alvin and I were speaking, and it's a wonderful idea, you and Henry, both your spouses passed on." She folds the dress and takes my right hand as if in a sisterhood, her thumb running over the wedding ring there. I say nothing to her assumptions, for that is exactly why I still keep the ring on that hand.

"I only told you where Marian's route goes. That's all I said." Alvin shakes his head.

"Honey." She turns her attention back to me. "You are so young. You deserve to love again, and you would make such a wonderful mother. Wouldn't she?" Her gaze shifts to Alvin, who nods once, slowly.

"No." I step to the side, trying to keep my mind from wandering to Rosalie's little face at the mention of being a mother. The last time she ran to greet me, she had tripped, skinning her knee. Jesse and Henry were still in the field, so I took water from a canteen Alvin had given me and washed the dirt and blood away. Her chin quivered as she sat in the dust, and I dried the knee by blowing gently upon it. When I healed it with a quick kiss, her face broke out in a smile, as if touched by magic, and she stood and reached for my hand. With her small fingers in mine, I knew this is what it must feel like, at least in a tiny portion, to be a parent. To have charge over a small soul, then be rewarded with grins and giggles. At the thought, my voice quivers as I answer Elleny. "No. Thank you, but no."

"He's a good man," Elleny plows on, looking quickly between the two of us, waiting for Alvin to back her up. "He can't see someone our age without offering them a hand or to carry their packages or groceries. You can always tell the best ones, you know, from how they treat those who can't do much in return. All give and no take, that man."

The whole time she talks, my head is shaking back and forth, though I don't dare speak up. Giving her opinion is Elleny's way of showing she cares, but unfortunately, showing her that you care in return generally means taking her advice. And this time I just cannot.

It would only be lying to myself if I didn't admit feelings for Henry have started. When my thoughts have nowhere to go, they find him. A few times, he has come in my dreams and now I lie awake in bed, unsure whether to be afraid to sleep or look forward to it, to be with him there. But I can't have him. I can't have him, or Rosalie, or even keep Alvin and Elleny, not so long as there is a target on my back.

My father's words echo in my ears, the words he thought I didn't hear. He'd only say them after the worst episodes, when he thought I was sleeping. His tall shadow would fill the doorway before he heel-toed those fancy shoes of his into my room and then sat the edge of the bed.

"*I love you,*" he would whisper into the air between us.

But I would always keep my eyes from fluttering and my swollen face turned away, only allowing tears to come when he had left the room. If broken ribs and arms covered in bruises is the price to pay for love, I want nothing of it.

"Surely you agree." Elleny's voice cuts into my thoughts.

Just then Alvin speaks up, his word gentle as a stream. "Elle, stop. Look at the girl."

For a moment, they both fall quiet as I feel their gaze and try to steady my hands that tremble. I swallow, suddenly aware of how short and quick my breaths have become, and how my heart rate picks up as though my father has stepped into the room. No matter how good they have been to me, if they try to pressure me into a relationship, I know I will go. All my life, I have heard people speak of how love is a sacrifice. If I were to stay and let myself fall in love, it would be sacrificing all I want from life. Love is only a rock you tie to yourself to help you sink.

"What is it that scares you, my dear?" Alvin whispers, his head tilting ever so slightly. Elleny places the dress in the chest and sits on the couch nearest her husband, then pats the cushion beside her for me to join them. She doesn't say a word, just smiles with wondering eyes, and I know she is ready to listen.

I sit on the edge of the cushion, though my back feels as though a rod were down it. "I suppose I should tell you." I chew on the inside of my cheek. "I don't intend to stay in Whitesburg forever. As soon as I'm on my feet, I must go."

The couple is still as they listen to my words. The only movement is Elleny reaching for Alvin's hand. It is Alvin who speaks up first.

"It is your husband you are running from, isn't it?"

I look down and don't answer, not desiring to lie to them, but also unable to speak the truth. Perhaps if Elleny believes I am wed, she will not press the matter of the pink dress anymore.

Alvin is shaking his head when I bring my gaze to meet his. "Whatever he has done to you, that is not love."

"Real love," Elleny interjects, squeezing Alvin's hand, "is beauty. True beauty."

"If you must go to be safe, we understand. But ask yourself if it's really necessary." Alvin chooses his words carefully.

"Don't go if it means you are running from something remarkable that could be yours. It's okay to be scared of love." Elleny seems to read my thoughts. "But don't let it stand in your way."

"It's hard, no excusing that." Alvin nods. "We all have our bad days. But it's worth fighting for."

"And sometimes," Elleny smiles over at her husband, the love right there in her eyes, "you win."

I look at them, their lovely skin aging together, and a longing washes over me in a wave. Of course I can't sit in their living room with them, see them holding hands with black-and-white framed memories covering the walls, and *not* want what they have. The longing is so strong, it feels as though I'm drowning, suffocating.

I can't live like this. I have to breathe free.

Yet . . .

I'm not ready to leave them. Not ready to walk away from this tiny haven where it feels like Warren can't reach me, where there is a warmth deep inside me that no chill wind could suck away.

I'm not ready to stop reading lessons with Rosalie, her head tucked into the crook of my arm, each of us holding a side of a book. Even if it means having to face that look in Henry's eye that leaves me feeling completely upended.

Someday I will go. Yes. Someday I will fill my pack and climb on Lady's back and never return.

But that day is not today.

Chapter Six

We lie in the hayloft, Rosalie and I, dining on hand-picked strawberries with a book between us. Our eyes have adjusted to the lighting of Henry's barn, and I can spot a couple of brown bats sleeping in the rafters. Through the open barn door, a wide shaft of light cuts through the dim, the air swirling with dust like pixies. Lengths of rope and baling twine dangle from nails on the weathered walls, and old leather tack is draped over stall railings. Though June is just beginning, it already smells of the summer, musky and sweet. The barn, though manmade, seems more nature than otherwise. It contains such life, such a vibrancy that I think I can almost hear the wild earth's heartbeat. *Here is a home in the way a nest is,* the earth whispers to me. *This is a place where one could learn to grow wings.*

"Everyone with good hands and feet came." Rosalie's story cuts into my thoughts. "It was like magic. In one day, the barn just *appeared!* And when it was done, we slaughtered a pig and roasted it over the fire, then Daddy took out his fiddle. We all danced and danced, and I stayed up late enough that Jesse showed me Orion and Draco in the sky."

I smile at her memory, but point to the book. "Come on, focus. What's this letter?" My finger rests on the easiest one to reel her back in.

"'R'! Like me!" She smiles like afternoon gold, with no restraint.

"That's right." I tug on a curl. "Like your name. Rrrrr. Now remember 'U'? What sound does it make?"

But we fall silent as the tired hinges on the russet-colored door yawn to life, and the shaft of light widens.

"But they're meant to be wild." Henry's voice breaks into the quiet. "And they *know it.* Ya see? They get what it's like to be free. So how could they ever be happy in there?"

"How about just till they get legs?" Jesse asks. "Not forever."

At the sound of their voices, I stiffen from head to toe. I suggested the barn to Rosalie solely for the purpose of hiding from them. From Jesse's disapproving looks . . . and Henry's looks that are undoubtedly *not* disapproving. The past few weeks, whenever I came for reading lessons, Henry's eyes would gain a spark and then he'd smile with each of his teeth showing. I couldn't watch his face light up like that without seeing again that moment my imagination had betrayed me, the thought of him holding my hand at the small porch table. Each time, I would drop my gaze, afraid that if he looked in my eyes long enough, he might see that moment in my thoughts, or worse, see me. *Truly see me.* And what then? What would he think of what he'd see? Would he cringe? I can't bear the thought. With anyone else, it doesn't matter to me, but with him, it's different. *He's* different.

But thinking like that will only bring trouble. My father is coming for me, I am sure of it, and as soon as I'm on my feet, I need to be off again. A small savings, some more new clothes, living arrangements a few towns over, and I'll be off and over the mountain before he can catch up to me. The longer he has to search, the angrier he must be becoming. I imagine Warren sometimes, those first few nights so sure I'd be around the next bend, so confident in his strength and cunning that it would be *simple*, he would have told himself.

Yet, it hasn't been. Each day that I've evaded him has been an insult to his capability, a knife swipe to his pride. Each day, the circle of where I could possibly be widens. But I know him. The longer it takes for him to find me, the worse it will be for me until perhaps there will be no limiting his anger. The only option is to run, run like a fire through the dry prairie, run like a madman, run until my lungs want to give out. Widen the circle until there are so many possibilities of where I could be that he could spend his life searching and never find me. Then, and only, I will breathe.

So for my part, when Henry smiles at me, I've tried to keep things fairly glacial between us. This way, nothing can grow. Sometimes I think I've made him successfully chilled, but then I'll fall into accents with Rosalie or celebrate a reading triumph with her and in my peripheral I'll see him, smiling still, turning his back so I won't see.

A glutton for punishment, that one.

So I started to find little nooks on the farm for us to take our lunch and practice, somewhere away from the sunlit porch and Henry's warm gaze. Yet here he is, and I know it's too much for Rosalie to stay quiet.

"Daddy!" she squeals, and crawls to the edge of the hayloft to peer down at him. With a sigh, I brace myself for the interaction. Men have always made me uncomfortable, but when Henry speaks, it's so much worse. I feel out of my skin, unsure what to do with my limbs.

"Hey, love! How's the lesson coming?"

But before she can answer, Jesse calls out, "Hey, Rosa! Come look at this! Tadpoles!"

Rosalie crawls back to me and grabs my arm as though he just said he stole a magic harp from a giant. "Tadpoles! Come on!"

She scales down the ladder, and I know I must follow. I may be hiding like a coward, but I certainly can't let them realize that.

Landing, I see Jesse first, a large jar balanced on his thin hip, little commas swimming around inside of it. The moment his eyes meet mine, his face contorts as if his insides are curdling and spoiling like milk with lemon. There's a parallel here I never have failed to notice—the more Henry takes a liking to me, the more Jesse looks at me like I'm something that would eat their own young. Henry can't cut me a slice of bread or hand me the pack of books without Jesse's face growing instantly darker. Then with smoldering eyes, he glares at me, and the message is clear. *Stay away! Go on, get.*

I will, I will, I want to say back. *Just not yet. Not quite yet.*

"Jesse, here," Henry says as he begins to unstrap the saddle from his horse. "Let Rosalie hold that for a second. Come on over here and get Rocinante some hay after all his hard work."

Rocinante.

I spin, my full attention on Henry. "What did you call your horse?"

Henry blinks twice, startled perhaps that rather than trying to disappear in the background as usual, I have turned on him. "Ro . . . cinante," he answers slowly, as though he's unsure what consequences will come from his simple answer, the horse nuzzling his ribs.

But *how?* My mind seems a spinning top, everything a blur. This man can't read more than a basic alphabet. How on earth does he know that name?

"Why?" My hands plead in front of me. "Why did you name your horse that?"

Henry looks at me as though I've asked to have my brain surgically removed. "It's the name of the horse in a bedtime story my father would tell me."

Ah. I exhale and nod. "Let me guess." I look at his beautiful red-and-white horse. "It was the tale of a delusional man who decides he is a knight, and attempts to revive chivalry and serve his country but mostly just makes one ridiculous error after another."

He tips his head to the side, and at last a bit of a smile plays on his lips. "Not quite. It was about a man who *knew* in his heart he was a knight, though no one believed him. Even though he was ridiculed, he held to that knowledge and behaved like the knight he was."

I fold my arms and look back at Henry. "Hmm. Seems your father took some liberties that weren't his place to take. *Don Quixote* is considered one of the greatest works of fiction ever written, a masterpiece. Your father should not have treated it so lightly." He may as well have painted a mustache on the *Mona Lisa*. The vandal.

Likely sensing tension, Jesse plops a pitchfork full of hay in front of the horse, and nudges Rosalie to follow him. Grabbing the tadpole jar, they slip from the barn, Rosalie turning at the doorway and giving us a little wave. I raise my hand and send her a soft smile, but turning back to Henry, my lips are again pinched straight.

But he's not looking at me at all.

"*Don Quixote.*" His gaze goes past me and he smiles, as

though an old friend was there that he hadn't seen in ages. "Let me ask you." He faces me again, and stepping forward, grabs hold of the horse's mane. "In the version you know, does he have a faithful squire named Sancho? Do they battle giants and find a healing elixir, then seek to lift an evil enchantment, all for the Princess Dulcinea?"

"Uh . . ." His questions make me pause, and I fiddle with a button on my peony dress. "Yes ... But no!" I shake my head. "Sancho is only a common laborer, and the giants aren't giants at all, just *windmills*. The 'elixir' actually makes Don Quixote sick, so that when he recovers, he only *believes* he has been magically healed. And Dulcinea was *never* a princess. Don Quixote convinced himself of that, but she is only a peasant woman!"

The horse's ears perk forward as my voice raises. As Henry listens, he just grins, lips closed but a contained laugh shaking his shoulders.

"I don't see what you find so amusing." I set my jaw, but Henry only seems to find that all the funnier. The laughter flows out of him, splashing against the worn barn walls. The laughter washes over me and makes me want to smile too, though I have no idea why. But I can't let Henry break down my walls that easily. I am stronger than that. With the possibility of laughing banished, I feel myself instead becoming infuriated.

"Why are you laughing?" I demand. "It's *a tragedy!*"

To that, he only laughs the harder. I fold my arms, trying to make myself an island.

"A tragedy? How could it ever be a tragedy?" His laughter subsides to chuckles, and he wipes a watery eye on the forearm of his sleeve. "It's about how a person can be right even while all of society is in the wrong, how a person can do what's honorable even if everyone else says there's no point."

"No." I raise my eyebrows. He did *not* just question me on my *Don Quixote* expertise. "It's about how we often do not see reality for what it is, for better or worse. Though Don Quixote's delusions imprison him, his imagination sets him free." I also grab hold of the horse's mane, as though he were the rope in a tug-of-war.

"I get the impression," Henry smiles, "that my father didn't *change* your version so much as he left out some elements. And it seems to me for the better."

For the better? My mouth falls open and I don't bother to shut it, don't bother to hide my disgust.

"But . . ." He takes a step closer, his voice slightly quieter. "I would like to compare the differences for myself. My father passed away shortly after I left home, and I have often wished I had found someone to help me write his story down."

"Not his—" I cut in, but Henry places a finger on my lips. I snap my mouth closed.

"I know, I know." His eyes are soft and gentle, his face still radiating so full of life from the deep laugh. He drops his finger, and I realize how close he is now standing. "It wasn't *his* story after all. But I would love to hear it again. It's been so many years, I know I've forgotten details. Please." He looks at me, this time with no laughter or even a smile, only pleading. "Do you know where I can find a copy? Does your packhorse library have any? Perhaps you could read it to us." Reaching down Rocinantes' mane, Henry rests his hand upon my own.

His touch is water on my fire, filling my mind with smoke too difficult to see through. I think of my book left resting on my pillow in Alvin's clean loft, about to be read again for perhaps the hundredth time. Then the treacherous imagining comes, each of their faces turned to me as

49

I read aloud, leaning forward on elbows, chins cradled in palms, and Henry's hand with my own, just as it is now.

Some things simply cannot be.

As I drop my hand from under his, the smoke stings my eyes and makes them tear.

"No." I look out the barn door so those deep eyes of his can't look through me and cringe to find my lie. "I'm sorry. I don't know where you could find it."

The lie swirls in the air about us along with the dust, and suddenly I feel as though I may suffocate on it all. Gazing down, I turn and escape through the barn door, the weight of their stares on my back. Away from Rocinante and his master, the man who fights for what he believes is honorable, whether he is wrong or not.

Chapter Seven

My feet hit the broken steps of Henry's cottage, water seeping through every stitch of my shoes. The pack of books is clutched to my chest cavity, my back arched to protect them from hail the size of hazelnuts. My skin is bruising, but this is nothing new to me. It's the delicate pages that must be safeguarded. The bag Henry gave me is good quality, made of hide from some animal and has always kept my books dry, yet today's storm seems to be taking that as a personal challenge.

When I left Alvin and Elleny's barn earlier, puddles rippled as if water sprites danced in them, and the thunder still sounded like a distant song. Already the air smelled of stone and wonder. On impulse, I had grabbed *The Call of the Wild* and shoved it in my bag, a tangible reminder that a soul can be stronger than the forces of nature. I knew the storm would likely get worse just looking at the clouds hugging the mountains, dark as a miner's kerchief. "I can do this," I'd whispered aloud just to feel the magic. I *had* to do this. It was reading lesson day.

Now the sprites that had danced instead stomp in their puddles, throwing tantrums. Lady whinnies behind me in protest to being left at the storm's mercy, the tree I left her under offering little safety from the ice marbles. I'll get her in the barn, but she can last a few more minutes out here while the books cannot. Reaching Henry's front door, I have to pound loud to be heard over the hail as it hits the roof like bullets.

My knuckles rap hard, and suddenly the door is flung open. Jesse stands there, the expression on his face instantly mirroring the sky. Behind him, I can see Henry in a rocker by the fire with Rosalie on his lap, both leaning forward to get a better look through the door.

"Marian!" Rosalie's eyes widen and she leaps from her father's lap, running at me with all the energy of a puppy. She bounds about me, attempts to jump into my arms, scampers off briefly to drag Henry over, and again bounds upon me, stopping just short, it seems, of actually barking. Despite the cold and the water running freely down my face, I have to smile. Every time I've come these last two months, she's been elated to see me, but this reaction, completely unfettered, makes the journey through the storm so worth it.

"You came in this unearthly weather? We figured you couldn't possibly be coming today." Henry clasps the door-frame and looks down upon me in surprise.

If Rosalie had been a pup, Jesse would be a defeated underdog. He has retreated to the fireplace, his tail between his legs and a muted glare over his shoulder.

"Come in, come in!" Henry beams. "I didn't recognize you at first. You look like you walked through a waterfall!"

"I'll soak your floor."

Henry laughs. "You don't need to worry about *that*. This isn't that kind of house."

He reaches out, and for a hummingbird second, his hand pauses before he places it on the small of my back and gently pushes me into the small cabin, lit with marigold light from the stone hearth. I tense as the warmth from his fingers travels through my thin wet dress, the gesture so foreign to me, it almost seems an invasion. Years were spent hoping for a gentle touch, and now that one comes, I don't know what to do with it.

But to my surprise, when his hand drops, so does something delicate and yellow in my heart. He looks at me with those quiet, dark eyes, as though waiting my command.

I don't want him, I remind myself. I want safety. That's all I've ever wanted. Freedom and wings and a chance to live life exactly as I choose. None of which I would get if I were to let him keep touching me.

"I'll see your horse into the barn." He holds my gaze in the way I imagine he would hold my shivering body, long and deliberate. But he steps outside without another brush of his fingers and I shake my head, forcing the daydream out, feeling again betrayed by my own imagination.

"What books did you bring this time?" Rosalie's fingers pry at the pack, and I let it spill open onto the oak table. Puddles are forming at my feet, but looking around, I see why Henry wasn't concerned about the mess. They may not have many worldly goods, yet everything they have sits out for every soul to see. Deer skulls and jars of wildflowers keep watch at the windows. Rather than electricity, they still have lanterns that spot the room, and a flat-bottomed bowl on the table contains several mismatched candles. Cast-iron pans hang on the walls, and a cutting board in the outline of a moose is propped above a window. There are two Native Indian rugs of bold red, black, and white, one on the floor and one hanging above the mantle. Above, thick wooden rafters protect it all. I only spot three photographs, no frames about them but instead nailed to the wall. From where I stand, it's difficult to make out the features in the black and white except for one—the portrait of a beautiful woman, the faintest smile on her lips.

"I have *The Velveteen Rabbit* and *Millions of Cats* to read to you." I pry my eyes from the picture and pull from the bag an empty cigar box Alvin gave me, which contains a few pencils for our lessons. "Ah, and we must not forget the good doctor, *Dolittle.* Then some old school primers for your practice—oh, *that* one is actually mine." My words cut off as she lifts the cover of *The Call of the Wild.* I know she can't possibly read something this difficult after only a few lessons, but her eyes stay hungry upon it, like a hunter just spotting an elk.

"Here, this one has pictures. Trade me." I try to place *Millions of Cats* between the girl and my book, attempting not to come across as a pouting toddler, the ferocious word "*mine!*" ready to pounce with vigor from my lips.

"What's so special about *that* one?"

Jesse's question cuts jagged into the small world between me and Rosalie. Our eyes turn to him as he strides over, shoulders rolled back like an alpha male. "We *don't want* your chicken scratch! It's no good! *Stop coming here!*" He snatches the book—*my* book—from Rosalie's hand and throws it with one sharp movement to the side. It hit the floor with a loud slap and slips toward the flames of the hearth while we can only watch it skid straight for destruction. I feel like a parent who has been told their child is ugly and dumb and should be left on the side of the street. I feel a justifiable sort of murderous. Finally, the book halts, stopping just a foot away from the fire, and I am able to exhale, able to react without total abandon.

My fingers curl around Jesse's forearm as I lower myself to his level. When my voice comes out, it is barely a whisper, but more fierce than a scream. "Besides children, books are *the most precious thing* on this earth." I breathe heavily with each word. "You are *never—never—*to treat one like that *again.*" His eyes are wide and his lips parted, waiting for a response that doesn't come. I shake his arm slightly, waking him from his stupor. "Give me your *word*, Jesse."

He nods once and bites his cheeks before answering. "Yes, ma'am," His words come out quick and timid and ten years old. He swallows, and guilt turns brown in my gut. I've scared the boy.

I lower my hand and try to make my voice gentle as I walk across the room and pick the book up from the wooden floor. "Books are 'no good,' huh?" I whisper. Sitting in the rocker, I meet the children's gazes, my fingers resting on the book in my lap. Their pairs of eyes watch me, the fire casting light over their features in the otherwise dim room. I reach my hand out to Rosalie, and she comes close to the rocker. "I believe that if anything in this world *is* good, if anything can make lasting change, it is *books.* Such as with slavery—no official document, no pretty speech, moved people so profoundly to change their opinions and see the evils in slavery as did *Uncle Tom's Cabin.* It laid the groundwork for the entire Civil War.

"Or look at you beautiful children. For ages, little ones like yourselves were sent to work in factories, under terrible conditions. Children were often injured and even died. Things began to change, however, when Charles Dickens wrote fictional books about such children, and called upon the hearts of the rich to remember that we are all one family and should care for those less fortunate." I notice that Jesse has taken a single step closer, and I lock eyes with him.

Jesse looks away from me and runs his fingernail in a grove on the table.

"Well? What have you to say to that?" I ask as Rosalie settles herself on my lap.

He shrugs with only one shoulder, not taking his eyes from the tabletop. I wait, and at last he mutters, "They still seem boring."

I blink in surprise at his comment, then can't help but laugh at the absurdity of it. The two of them look at me in shock, wordless as my laughter rolls over them and slowly ebbs, leaving only the sound of the heavy rain on the tin roof in the room. Leave it to children not to care if books were important enough to start a war—they must have their *own* worlds rocked.

Lifting the book in my hand, I curl my other arm around Rosalie. "Let's see if this sounds boring to your brother, shall we?"

I look into Rosalie's bright face, but now I am speaking to Jesse. "A domesticated dog, Buck, is living on a ranch in California when he is *stolen* from his home and sold to be a sled dog in brutal Alaska. He has to rely on his primitive instincts to become a leader in the wild. But . . ." I pause for dramatic effect, and open to a page I once marked simply because of how it spoke to the depths of me.

> "'Deep in the forest a call was sounding, and as often as he heard this call, mysteriously thrilling and luring, he felt compelled to turn his back upon the fire and the beaten earth around it, and to plunge into the forest, and on and on, he knew not where or why; nor did he wonder where or why, the call sounding imperiously, deep in the forest.'"

I could go on and on, and I see in their fixed eyes that

they want me to. Even Jesse, who had always avoided the books like a dead body, draws close enough that he is now only a few steps away.

With that, I close the book and look the young boy square in the eye.

"These words speak to me because I know that feeling, of having nature calling to something deep inside me that proper civilization would smother." I pause and reverently run my fingers along the golden engraved title of the book.

"*This* is why I read. Contrary to popular belief, it is not to escape, to forget about life." The storm pounds away with all its vigor, and speaking over it gives my words a strength, something solid for me and the children to cling to. "Just as an actor who never knows grief can't hope to convey it on stage, so can a person only love reading for what the pages reflect back about life. For the feelings they capture that nothing else can, the chance to see your own thoughts—but someone else's words—on paper and be able to say, 'Yes! That's *exactly* how it feels!' You see? It gives value to the small moments. It puts weight onto the things that would float away from us." I lift a cupped hand as though holding something carefully, then look up as if it were a ladybug flying off. Rosalie pulls on a lock of my russet hair, tickling my cheek with it, and I smile at her before going on.

"That's only its *first* gift." I look at Jesse now, and know he will understand better what I speak of next. "In a world that would want to sink its teeth into you and rip you into pieces, it gives you a weapon." As he listens, I can see something different in him. Something in how his eyebrows are raised, in how his jaw is slack. "*Imagination.* Here started all the hope, all the dreams, all the triumphs I have ever known."

"But they're just stories," Jesse whispers, but the anger in his voice is gone. "Made up."

Just the tiniest bit, I feel my head shake.

"It doesn't matter if the character really lived or if they were made up in some stranger's mind. For a character is only the handful of traits their author gives them, and then we get to look at that individual and see their story and know, '*That* is what I want to be like. *I have that in me too.*' All the best individuals—real or made up, human or animal —" I hold up the book. "—give us someone to look to and say, 'Because of *you*, I didn't give up." At last I break the trance between us and rest my head on the rocker, my eyes finding the wooden rafter beams. "And *that* is how I made it through the storm."

I know he's thinking of the hail shower. That too.

"Well . . ." His eyes watch the lick of the flames in the hearth. "Maybe *that* book isn't too boring."

I chuckle and run my fingers over Rosalie's curls, working out a knot.

"Will you read it to me?" His voice could come from a different boy altogether.

My fingers wrap around the book, and I don't take my other hand from Rosalie's hair. The boy is waiting for a smile, for a joyful "yes." But I can't.

"No." I meet his eyes. We stare at each other just a moment, my heart tripping on a beat. Then, just as I see his jaw start to become set again, I drop my hand from his sister's hair and with both hands, offer the book to the boy. "You will."

He doesn't touch it, just eyes it with suspicion as a pack would a newcomer. I cling so tightly to the book that I can feel my pulse in my fingertips, but my hand stays outstretched. He can't possibly know how much this pains me, how much I want to pull it back to my racing heart and tell him I'll bring him another. But I know that this is my chance. Right now, in this moment, his heart is open. If I wait even a day, my little plea will become only a memory, and the demands of the farm will consume this young boy again. But this book, this scuffed-up, faded, beautiful book has begun to work its magic on the boy's thoughts, on his heart. I will leave today, but this will stay, calling to the boy as the wilderness did to Buck. Thrilling and luring, reminding him that he has this in him.

"I could never read that. It's not easy like the books you bring Rosa."

Smiling again, I nod and stretch it out farther. "It would likely take you *years* to learn how to read this. But it's in no hurry—Buck will be waiting on your shelf. A story is one of the only things never to age. If you work hard, each day you will get better. When the day comes that you pick it up and it can speak back to you, then you could read just about anything. Will you take it, Jesse? Will you do this?"

He doesn't respond, but someone else does.

"We'll read it together." Henry stands in the frame of another room. There must be a backdoor through there, for all our heads jerk at his voice. He strides toward us, the silver feeling in my veins returning, and he sinks to one knee in front of the boy, resting a strong hand on his shoulder. "You won't have to learn alone. We'll make the time, even if it means quizzing each other on our letters while we work in the barn. We aren't afraid of a little hard work, are we?" He grins at the boy, a challenge between father and son.

At last the boy reaches out, and for the briefest moment, both our hands are on the book. I wonder if I really can let it go. *I can do hard things*, I tell myself, the same words that got me through my other storms. This should be easy in comparison, yet when was giving up a piece of your soul ever that simple? But I just said it, didn't I? The only thing more precious than books is children. He is worth it.

Letting go, the magic of the words already begins its magic.

Jesse actually smiles.

Suddenly there is a deafening crack, followed by frantic brays. The children and I dash to the window, but Henry is already on his feet and out the door. A large branch has broken from a tree, punching in the barn door as if it were a boxer's tooth. Through the open doorway, I can see Lady out of the limb's reach, but Rocinante, terrified, bolts out. Henry waves his arms, the muscles in them taut, his feet sliding in the mud as he tries to keep the horse from charging into the forest.

"We have to go help him!" Jesse cries, tossing the book on the table and scampering for his shoes. "The other animals will get out if we don't!"

Rosalie and I nod, but as they rush out, I pause in the doorway, eyes falling on the discarded book on the table, its spell broken. I wonder what will come of it, if perhaps my sacrifice was a waste.

Not a thought in their minds is on it anymore. Reality wins. The farm and the storm take the prize.

Closing the door on the simple bound book, I wonder if they truly will pick it up again.

Chapter Eight

The sun is smashed red and flat along a cloudless horizon as I make my way into town, my pack empty for the day. Below, the town is a few minutes ride away, and with each of Lady's dusty steps, I dream of washing away the July heat with a cool bath.

Suddenly, I notice a figure step from the trees to the middle of the road and turn toward me, waiting. The sun glares at my eyes and I squint, trying to make out the stranger's attributes. It's rare that I see other travelers on this road, and dread pushes against me like a fierce wind as I pull on Lady's reins, slowing us as I attempt to get a better look.

"Marian!" The shadow waves arms above its head, and I recognize the voice as Alvin's. I would feel relieved, but there is a stiffness in how he stands that makes me think this isn't a social visit.

"Alvin! Why aren't you at the post office?" I call, digging my heels into Lady's sides to get me to Alvin quick. "Whoa!" Stopping Lady, I dismount, and the first thing I notice as I face Alvin is the alarm in his eyes.

"A man has come to town, asking for you." Alvin grabs at Lady's reins as he says the sentence that every day I have feared I would hear. "Tall." Alvin jerks his head up, as though looking high above his own. "Light brown hair. Nice suit. He stood out, wearing something like that in this heat, so I quieted myself when he came in and heard when he asked the postmaster for a Marian Kearnes. He introduced himself as Warren Kearnes and described you. Then the postmaster—the dolt—said he thought he'd seen you working for *me*."

Fear claws at my insides, an animal frantic to get out, but my face is set as if by rigor mortis, teeth locked together tight.

"He came to my desk, and I fed him a story. That you *had* come looking for a job, but the position had just been filled. I told him that I advised you to look into a teaching job I'd heard of a few towns over." He shakes his head. "But Elleny says I'm a terrible liar, that I don't have enough practice for anyone to believe me. He left, but he could still be in town. He's the trouble you're running from, isn't he?"

I nod once, stiff, the only sound the cicadas clipping around us.

"We can't take the streets. Come on, I'll get you home through the forest." Jerking on Lady's reins, he begins to guide the way.

"I can't." I grab on to my mare's saddle, and she halts at my touch. "Warren knows you are his best lead. He will ask around and find out where you live. If he finds me in your barn and learns how you have helped me, he will take it out on you, I know it." I exhale slowly, wiping hair from my eyes. "He's done it before."

"Marian—"

"He's bound to be especially furious, he doesn't react

with sense when he gets like that. It would be wrong to put you both at risk." I think of the vinegar-lipped woman who gave up this job. If Warren spoke to her, he would know I took the position here, and this is the town he's been looking for. "I have to go. He'll find me here . . ." Panic creeps up my throat, twisting my voice. In my mind I see faces, faces I will never see again, but I push them away. I can't let myself even think of them right now.

"Wait! You can't start from square one again. You have a job here, a place to stay. In this economy, that isn't something to take for granted. Is there somewhere you can lie low, just for a few days, until he moves on? One of the mountaineer families you've made friends with?"

No, no, he's wrong. All that matters now is freedom, and that won't happen if I let myself get cornered. Warren knows I'm not far. When I think of him, I picture him almost sensing me, moving slowly but with purpose, the hairs up his spine rising just knowing I'm close. It's only a matter of time.

Unless I run. I've started with nothing before, and it proved to me that I can do it again. Besides, the moonless night doesn't scare me like it used to—well, as least not to the point of desperation. I know the mountains now—I no longer feel as though I'm trying to survive on Jupiter. It would be difficult, to travel by day eating only the plants Alvin has shown me as safe and spend my nights sleeping with no blanket but the stars, but I spent enough days starving to make up my mind. I would rather die this way, a wild, cageless creature with the entire heavens open before me, than live with Warren's grip making me powerless, like a pup lifted by the skin of the neck.

For Alvin's sake, I nod. "Yes, I can figure this out," and he believes I'm agreeing with him.

He exhales, his head bobbing up and down as he

thinks. "You can still earn money if you keep working. I'll come here and leave some food, one of your outfits from the barn, and your daily book load behind this boulder." He motions to the side. "He won't stay long when there's no sign of you. It will be okay."

Yellow tightens like ribbons around my ribcage as I imagine Alvin's face when he returns to this rock in a couple of days and sees his carefully prepared package for me left untouched. He'll know then what I did. I want to tell him now, to give a proper goodbye, but as much as I want to trust the graying man, I know it would leave a trail for Warren to follow. There can be *no* possibilities for Warren to pursue.

But oh, Alvin has been so good to me.

Reaching out, I clasp his papery hand in my own, feeling the bones as fragile as a bird's and the knuckles slightly swollen with age. "Thank you, Alvin." I smile, and blink to keep a tear from falling. "Thank you for giving me this job and believing in me. You took a total stranger in! I've been the happiest here that I've been in my whole life, and that wouldn't be if it weren't for you." The tear careens down my cheek, and I turn my face as though looking at the town to avoid letting him see it.

"Everything is going to be fine." He squeezes my hand, the lines on his face soft as spider webs.

I let go.

We look at each other, young and old, woman and man. I don't say goodbye. But to him, I actually could. "You're a good friend," I whisper to keep the emotion from being pronounced in my voice. Saying more might reveal my plan, so I mount Lady and turn the horse back up the mountain.

Looking over my shoulder, I see that Alvin's silhouette hasn't budged. He raises one hand and holds it high for a moment. I return a wave that's far more cheerful than I feel inside.

Then facing forward, I ride into freedom.

The reins shake in my trembling hands, and I breath in the night air deeply to steady myself. I expect the sweet and rich smell of pine and magnolia to fill me, but the dryness of the last days has left the scent bland and unsatisfying.

Snapping the reins to go faster, my mind goes back to the small home I've made in the loft of Alvin's barn. No fewer than six quilts were stacked on hay bales for my bed, and on top of a crate sits an oil lamp and my two remaining books. In the evenings when the lamp was lit, I would read my old books or some I'd borrow from the WPA library, and think to myself that perhaps contentment is the most marvelous feeling of all. To want nothing, to live only in gratitude for what the moment has to offer. Even if it is just the turning of a page in a glow as soft as the inside of a cocoon.

But now that's behind me. I left the top quilt turned down, the pair of britches I bought with my own money across the end of the bed, and *Don Quixote* propped open, waiting to face the windmill giants. I shed it all like a snake sheds its skin, a piece of itself, yet discarded and never to be returned to again.

"Yah!" I call to Lady, leaning into her mane as though we can outrun my thoughts. I try to imagine in order to give myself strength. *I am a gypsy. A nomad. A vagabond.* My eyes dart to the trees surrounding us. The titles sound exotic, and for a moment, the allure of adventure seems to peek out and beckon through the pines in front of me. "Come on, girl!" I urge, as if it is a nymph that will escape us.

For a moment, with the night air chilling my skin as I ride and the sound of cicadas louder than a jungle drum, I feel it. I can ride through the night in one direction and see what new adventure the day will bring. Now, with possibilities about to dawn on the other side of the mountain, I realize how many tiny, invisible threads were being tied to me as I stayed there. Much longer, and they'd be enough to tether me to the ground, as simple ropes do to a grand hot air balloon.

I was not made to be tethered. Of this I am sure—I was made to soar.

Coming to the ridge of the mountain, I bring Lady to a trot. Her sides heave under my legs, and when we hear water rushing over stone, we turn toward it. The distance now between myself and the town—and therefore Warren —have made me feel like the boa constrictor around my chest has loosened its grip so I can breathe again.

Climbing down, I kneel on the bank, cupping the cool water in my hands where it seems to be running the fastest. We drink side by side for a long time, elegant animal and I, then I stand and look down the mountainside we just rode. Lights of cabins speckle across the black face of it, like an upside down night sky. Most of the homes were on my route, and as my eyes flit from one to the next, I remember each face. Their children would come running to the horse, then they'd invite me in for coffee, and adults and children alike would tell me about the books they'd finished in such detail, it was as if I'd read them myself. Once in a while as I left, they'd give me the only "thank you"s they had. A poke of berries. A family pie recipe passed down from mother to daughter through the generations. By now, there wasn't so much as a pet dog in the family that I didn't know on a first-name basis. They called me "that book lady" at first, then later when asked for my proper name, I'd stoop to the children's level and insist in some English accent that "That Book Lady" is a very proper name, thank you very much, and couldn't fit me better if me own mum had named me that. So it stuck.

Only Henry's family called me Marian.

At last my eyes fall on the light from his cabin, and I know my gaze has been avoiding it. My mind will no longer allow their faces to stay buried in my subconscious, and they push to the front.

Rosalie, her usually smiling features intent and still as she would give all her focus to each letter she was practicing.

Jesse. Oh, Jesse, who always has to act so very grown. Yet now his face softens when he sees me, and he holds the door open wide in silent invitation when I come.

Henry.

The wind caresses strands of hair onto my cheeks, and I brush them back without taking my eyes from the small lit cabin.

I can picture Henry so easily there, always quick to give Rosalie's curls a tousle, or Jesse a nudge with his elbow. Then he'd feel my gaze on him and he'd turn, smiling before our eyes even met. Each time, he would keep those deep dark eyes locked with mine, as if he was waiting for me to say something first. But I would just look away instead.

This mountain has a new wonder growing around each rock, shaking on the tree limbs. Yet this tiny log cabin, Navajo rugs on the walls and wildflowers plucked for the windows, seems the most wondrous of all. Though it is modest, there is something pulsating, alive yet unseen, that resonates in those walls. Something indestructible.

I pry my eyes from the cabin and turn back to Lady. It's not five steps and we can already see over the edge of the mountain and to the other side. A beautiful unknown.

Lady nuzzles my arm, and I stroke her soft fur, feeling

as though I am standing on some thin line. Freedom—bold and salty and made up of pure adventure on one side.

Purpose, hearth glow, and that indestructible something on the other. But as tranquil as it sounds, that is where my captor waits.

Yet I pause. And the longer I stand here, the more that line seems to disappear beneath my feet. My mind grows fuzzy like static, as taking steps one direction or the other would bring that line back with clarity.

Still facing my mountainside, I look over my shoulder to the valley on the other side. For so long, that has been all I've wanted. To follow uncharted roads, to not see a road sign for miles, to be the captain of my own soul. My need for this is like my desire for each next breath—constant, without need for explanation. The decision should be automatic.

But then I think of Henry, home with the children, eating around the table he built himself. This cabin, this small speck in the whole wide world, that I can't seem to pull my eyes from. Wind pushes against my back, pulling my dress against my legs, as though bidding me to come back down the mountain.

I want to be there. I want to be who I am when I am there, going where I'm going, when I'm not going anywhere at all. Taking a step, the line at my feet comes into focus. I will not cross it, not tonight.

It's not safe. It's not freedom.

But maybe it's an adventure all the same.

Chapter Nine

For three days, the dread stayed with me at all times, a spider with tiny feet leaving a trail of silk along my spine. Each day I'd retrieve the bundle Alvin left for me and try to make myself appear presentable after spending a night under the stars. I could have asked the mountaineer families if I could stay with them, but that placed them in the same position Alvin and Elleny had been in. I could not bring danger to their doorstep.

So I took my sweet time on the route each day, visiting with each family as long as possible until the lighting of lanterns in their electricity-lacking homes signaled that it was time to let them settle in for the night. I'd found a splotch of earth with no advantages other than good visibility in case of danger, and attempted to make a bed there of pine needles and thick grasses. Laying there, I watched the moon disappear a fingernail clipping at a time, telling myself if cowboys could do this, so could I.

'Course, they had guns. But I tried not to dwell on that fact.

Instead, I told myself stories, understanding now why those cowboys were always known for their campfire tales. Without the warmth of companionship or fire, I could only tell them to myself, and my thoughts would always drift back to those three precious tales that were worth running away with.

Closing my eyes against the dark, I'd see Dorothy and her odd friends searching for bravery and a heart. Placing my fingers over my own heartbeat, I'd recall almost every page until at last my slippers would remind me that I already have with me the very things I wish to obtain—and what I don't have, the journey will instill in me.

Inevitably, the scratch on bark of an unseen creature would make my eyelids fly open and body stiffen as I rehearsed scenarios in my head of how I would hope to survive a bear attack. Running my hands across arms prickled from terror and cold, my thoughts would call, as if with a whistle, for Buck to come protect me. Through the shadows of the night, he would sprint until his story was there full force. He and I are not so different. Gone is a world of comforts, but in the wild, something beckons to us. *Come,* the still earth whispers. *I know things that you do not. Let me show you. Let me show you the unknown, yet the truer part of your own self.* Lying there, craning my senses to understand the rocks and the breeze and the plants that sway, wishing to know not from books, but from experience what the earth taught Buck. That inside of me, there is an unconquerable something.

If these lessons are lies, they are the loveliest lies, the lies worth believing in. When doubt would say otherwise— that I do *not* have an invincible force inside me, stronger than anything against me—I would remember Don Quixote. In a reality where chivalry is dead and you are mocked as a fool, you alone can say you are more than that. How I loved Don Quixote for his fierce belief in the impossible on those nights. I felt unhinged, positive that Warren watched from the bushes for my eyelids to close, and then reality would come flooding back to me. The only world I've ever known, where each day I'm told that I am worthless and weak, and each blow attempts to reinforce it. Where a whisper reminds me that I am only a motherless child, unfit for even a father to love.

But Don Quixote! He begs me to ask, does fact really weigh more than belief? I cannot, particularly during these cold nights with only pine needles for a bed, let myself believe that. A chance taken *is* more valuable than a chance you pass up. Love *is* more important than power, good *does* conquer evil, myth *can* matter more than history, someone can leave you *and* still love you. If these are falsehoods my fairy tales have deluded me into believing, I would rather spend my life living a lie than pay homage to a repulsive truth. I am not ignorant, as my stomach claws at its own sides from hunger, as I seek sanctuary among the bears and mountain lions, that life can take you by the throat until you turn blue and your lips plead for wordless mercy. But I do know that this mind God above gave me is a place of its own. It can, if trained and harnessed and reined in like the wildest of mustang, be the best weapon I have for fighting back.

I'd tell myself this every night. Sometimes, by dawn's first restless cracks of light, I could convince myself these beliefs were true. Or if not true, then at least all that mattered.

But sometimes I couldn't.

Either way, on those nights, sleep made up its mind to have nothing to do with me. No matter how lovely the lies I tell myself, three days with *no* sleep is a fabulous way for anyone to get in touch with the crazed side of themselves.

Between that and the knowledge that Warren was close, by this third day, my nerves are worn to the quick. Like any trait, the flip side of my imagination is a curse, insisting that every snap of twig is either some monstrous animal akin to a yeti, or the monster I had faced growing up. I haven't dared let my guard down enough to bathe in a river, so now black crusts the edges of my fingernails and a thick grit covers every inch of me, even my teeth. I can no longer seem to get my thoughts to behave as I want. Like an amateur learning the fiddle, try as I may, they screech rather than soothe.

But still, I pick up the bundle Alvin left me, then Lady and I turn up the mountain path. Leaning into her neck, I let her follow the path she knows so well, and though I don't feel the energy to smile, a sunset-orange fills my chest. This is the day I've been counting down toward. Lessons day.

Through the trees, I see Henry's cabin, the lights inside still lit as dawn is starting to come later and later. It's my first stop today. I can't bring myself to wait for lunch, and I know they won't be expecting me for hours still. Yet I need to be in that home like I need a medic, as though I don't know if I'll go on otherwise.

It doesn't surprise me to see Henry out front, circles of tree trunks scattered around him waiting to be split. He's stacking the wood that's all set for winter as I ride up, each placed as meticulously as if it were a house of cards. When he hears me, he turns, wiping the sweat from his forehead with his arm and blocking the dawn's light to see my face better.

"Marian?" He smiles. It feels so good to hear him say my name.

Riding up next to the porch, I swing my leg over and try to dismount. My dress gets in the way and my limbs don't respond fast enough until I'm falling fast to the dusty earth.

"Whoa!" I hear Henry cry out, and as I brace myself for impact, instead I feel his arms surround me. Both of our breaths are heavy, our faces close, and Henry kneels, having caught me just in time.

For once, I don't fight his touch—I haven't the strength. Chest heaving with fear, that whole dam of fear breaking at the sudden fall, I lean my head into the crook of his neck and swallow down tears.

Lifting my chin with a finger, he meets my damp eyes. "What has happened to you?" he whispers, a crease of concern etched on his face.

I just shake my head, tucking it back into his neck, knowing if I were to speak out loud, my whole reservoir of strength would burst.

Without another word, he lifts me in his strong arms and carries me into the house, setting me in the rocking chair by the hearth. "I'm going to tie up Lady. You just hang tight. Rosalie wasn't feeling well last night and kept Jesse up, but they should be awake any minute," he says, his hand on the back of the rocker and his eyes on my level, then stands and steps out.

My eyes land on the portrait of the beautiful woman I spotted before, but this time it has been taken from the wall and set on the table, along with a dirtied breakfast plate, and I understand Henry must have been holding it, *holding her*, not even an hour ago as he ate. In the black-and-white shades, I can tell this is where Jesse gets his bleach-blond hair, and it flows straight down her back nearly twice the length of my shoulder-length auburn waves. I pick up the portrait and meet her soft eyes, painfully aware of the slight part in her lips that I realize Henry knows so well. Looking at her, I suddenly feel out of place, lonely as a tumbleweed, unwanted anywhere in this world.

Henry walks back in, carrying a large metal basin for bathing, and I hastily set the photo back down while his back is turned closing the door. "If you're comfortable with it, I can set this up in the kids' room so you can have some privacy when they wake. I'll get heating some water right now, then it will only take a minute to fry up an egg and toast for ya." He is rushing, but one look at me and he stops in place. There must be something in how I lean away from the photo, something in the look on my face, or in the way the picture has been moved, that tells him everything he missed. With a soft smile, he walks over and picks up the portrait, then places it back on the empty nail on the wall.

"Her name was Rae. I was thinking, I still have a few dresses of hers that should fit you just fine. You can't be going and putting that back on once you're all washed up."

"Oh, no." I shake my head. "I couldn't. That's what you have left of her. There's no chance I could possibly take those from you."

Moving the breakfast dish to the table, Henry sits in the chair, then to my surprise, he reaches out and takes my hand in his. "Please. It would be good to see them being used again." His hold is soft, yet firm and confident, like a worn saddle, and when I meet his eyes, I see he is smiling. I search them for the pain that I know comes from loving, but right now he's just looking at me, not a thought divided.

"You must miss her very much," I manage, slowly pulling my hand away.

"I do." He nods once, but doesn't take his gaze from mine. "It *has* been four years, though." He pauses then, and looks at the wedding ring on my right hand, his face suddenly becoming more grim. "Ah. How long has it been for you?"

My eyes drop to the diamond ring, and I spin it with my thumb. "Twenty-three years."

At Henry's shocked reaction, a soft swell bubbles up inside of me. "I never married—it was my mother's. She's been gone since I was just a tiny thing." As always, the words send ice water through my veins.

He nods slowly. "You're like my kids. You know what it's like to lose a mother."

I've heard that word a lot over the years. "Lose." As if I just misplaced her, by accident.

Forcing myself to look at Henry, the words come out quiet, each one an effort. "There's a big difference between *lost* and *left*."

He jerks back as though I pulled a gun on him, then quickly rearranges his features to pity. "Oh, Marian." He leans forward, eyes locked on my face.

My gaze turns to rest on the ashes in the hearth, but I can still feel the weight of his stare. I swallow, feeling empty as a ghost town, as the story comes. "I always told myself she *had* to go, that she wouldn't possibly leave me by choice with such an angry father. I'd imagine that there was some big fight between them, that she had to run for her life or he'd kill her." In my mind, I could see her pulling the ring from her finger and throwing it to the floor as fury curdled blood red in his eyes. "It could have happened like that." I pause, and feel my breath come out slow and shaky. "Of course, that very well could just be one of those pretty lies I make myself believe." Don Quixote and me, always deluding ourselves.

"And this ring is all you have left from her?" Henry's eyebrows draw together.

Lifting my eyes, I tip my chin toward the shelf where

The Call of the Wild watches over us right next to the water
pitcher. "And three books." Henry is on the edge of his seat
now, so close I can smell the breath of pine on him from
chopping wood. "My father kept them to himself. When I
was about Rosalie's age, I found the ring with the books
tucked above his wardrobe, and I knew they must have
been hers. I *had to* know what those books said. I thought
maybe they contained a secret message from her to me." I
scoff slightly and run my fingernail through a grove in the
arm of the rocker. "From then on, I was on fire with reading, and for years I would sneak out the books and ring
whenever I was certain my father would not catch me.
Through the years, he had no idea that I've read them over
and over. Up until a few months ago."

Henry's gaze is fixed steady on my face and he reaches
out, gently resting a hand on my knee. "What happened a
few months ago?" His touch is so soft, not demanding but
asking permission, and this time I don't pull away.

"He said he was going to deliver supplies that came to
the store for a farmer who had broken a leg and couldn't
come in to pay. I waited until I was positive he was gone,
but maybe I had gotten too lax. Or maybe he was already
on to me, and crept back quietly. I don't know. But he
found me just as I'd pulled the box down from the
wardrobe." The memory spins, churning my stomach in a
vile kaleidoscope. He looked at me like I needed an exor-
cism, then his features hardened into rage. "He was always
angry about something, but I'd never seen him look at me
like *that*. And I knew as he came for me that he was going
to kill me." I exhale, long and heavy, as I remember the
attack, wild and unrestrained. "And he certainly tried," I
whisper.

As I speak, Henry looks at me with eyes intense, yet
peaceful, like the land after a storm. Only the thumb

holding my hand moves, and he slowly strokes it across my knuckles. I pause for a moment and watch our two hands together. Everything in my past screams at me not to trust the touch of a man, not to let that simple touch travel up my arm and into my heart. If not for me, for him. The only other times in my life that I've tried to use young men as an escape, Warren found out, then ended it with a message. An injured horse. A fire in the barn. No one could prove it was him, but we knew.

He's done it before, and he's close now. I shouldn't do this to Henry.

And yet there is something so strong, so sure in his gentle touch, that instead I find my fingers curling around his own, as if he were an anchor. With a deep breath, I continue my story.

"He threw me to the ground, right by the fireplace, and I grabbed a handful of hot ash with my bare hands and smashed it into his face." The memory comes alive as I tell it in full detail. I remember how he started to lift me by the throat as my hand swung from the fireplace, searing pain down my arm. Then suddenly I was dropped to the floor as he flew back howling, both hands covering his face. Like the story I'd told myself of my mother, I knew this well could be my only chance to be free. "When he let go, I knew I had to run away for good. The books and ring lay at my feet in their box, and I scooped them up as I ran to the door." I remember hugging them to me, as though they were my children, and then seeing Lady in a field nearby. "One of our horses, my favorite, Lady, wore her reins and saddle. He must have been taking her to that farmer's. I flew to her as fast as I could, but my father was on my heels, cursing and screaming. His fingers grasped some of my hair, but when he tried to yank me back, I thrust my head forward." I remember how my head throbbed from the hairs pulled out by the roots, and for a moment, my vision clouded in pain. "I mounted Lady and we took off without looking back. I rode for miles, after the sun set, until Lady had to stop."

My gaze lifts from our hands as I meet Henry's eyes. "The next person I saw was you."

He tilts his head, the corner of his lips raising on one side. Lifting his free hand, he tucks one of my stray hairs behind my ear. "Thank you for telling me," he whispers.

I nod once, the thoughts of Warren—thick in my mind. His fists left their lasting bruises on my memory, leaving my soul black and blue. And his eyes, distant and scorching as a desert sun, seem to remain at all times in the back of my mind with absolute clarity.

Sitting here with Henry, I want to believe he is different. Yet there always remains the knowledge that at times, it was Warren who was different. As much as I want to paint him black, the villian with nothing redeemable, most of our days were spent in the gray. He was never what most people would call affectionate, but he'd always make sure the store that he ran was stocked with my favorite sweets, and not once did I go without a meal. He bought me fine clothes and sat by the bed when I was sick.

Or otherwise recovering.

Perhaps there is no one alive who doesn't have some good in them, but the other side of the coin insists that there is no one alive who doesn't have some wicked in them. Warren showed me that anyone can hide their crazy for a while. I'm certain Mama didn't see it when he first put this ring on her finger just five months after they had met. How soon after the wedding day did the beatings start? She became his marionette, and he controlled all the strings.

Looking down at my hand that Henry holds, I can almost see the strings tight around each finger.

Loosening my hold, I pull my hand from him and into my lap as my gaze falls to the floor.

"So now you understand why I can't be with anyone. It isn't safe."

I expect him to drop his other hand from the side of my face, but he doesn't. Instead, his thumb caresses my jawline as he dips his head to catch my eyes.

"I understand that the people who shoulda shown ya what love is did a poor job of it. Not everyone is like that."

He reaches his other hand up until both cup my face. How I want to believe him. Tears well in my eyes and I pinch them shut to keep them from spilling over. I shake my head the tiniest bit, and feel his fingers softly press into my cheeks. "I can't."

"Your father isn't here. He can't stop you anymore."

I shake my head my fiercely, about to insist, *No, he is here, he's in town.* But if he weren't, would it change anything?

"Marian," His voice is soft, but without any more words commands me to be still. Forcing myself to open my eyes, I see Henry. His dark curls are an unruly mess, and his plain blue shirt has flecks of wood stuck to it. His jawbone is defined and clean cut. His nose may be a bit too large to be perfect, but perhaps his beauty despite imperfection is what holds me so mesmerized.

And here he is, looking at me. Leaving me feeling like I've warmed in summer's rays, like I am *someone.*

But the bitter aftertaste of my story is still heavy on my tongue, and I know that if my parents taught me anything, it is that love is pain. I'm not so young and naive as to believe otherwise. Isn't love always described as a flame? Of this I am sure—I have been burned enough.

"No." My voice comes out firm this time. "I can't."

For a moment, Henry doesn't move but for his eyes, which study my face with intent. Finding an answer there, he drops his hands and stands. Without looking at me again, he heads to the kitchen and pulls out a large metal pot. "We're on well water. I'll go get some for your bath." He opens the door, then pauses, the morning light pouring through. "That book was one of the only things you had of your mother's, and you gave it to us. Why?"

His question catches me off guard, and I shrug. "I have just about every page memorized. You and your family need it more than I do."

"Exactly." He nods. "I'll put Rae's old dresses on the chair in that room." He smiles so soft, those beautiful dark liquid eyes meeting mine. "I may not be much of a reader yet, but this much I've learned. No matter how you feel about one chapter, whether you love it or hate it, rereading it over and over won't do you a bit of good. You have to keep reading to find out how the story ends."

He hesitates, waiting for an answer.

I can only look up at him, bathed in that morning light, and know that to let myself love him would be like flying into the sun. "Henry." I shake my head. "It's not that I don't want to. I just *can't.*"

Our gaze stays bound for a moment, then without a word, he walks through the door and closes it behind him.

Chapter Ten

There's a terrible nothingness in the quiet with him gone and the children still sleeping out of sight, as if the breath left a living creature and it lies disturbingly still. I sit in the rocker. unsure what to do with myself. After our conversation, I'm tempted to stand, open the door, and finally cross that invisible line in the mountains. Up and over to the other valley. Perhaps staying was the wrong choice. Perhaps it's the wrong choice even now.

But the idea of a warm bath is a powerful one. If I don't endure a bit of awkwardness and take this opportunity to get clean, the dust will be so thick on me, it could feel like fur.

"Daddy." Rosalie's voice comes from the other room, but something is off about it. *Oh, yes*, I recall. *Henry said Rosalie had been sick all night.* I would answer that he just stepped out—it feels strange to roam the house that isn't mine—but how could I leave the sweet girl comfortless? Rising from the chair, I go to the children's doorway and immediately am struck with the pungent smell of vomit. There's no window in the room, and it takes a moment for my eyes to adjust to the lack of light. Along one wall, Jesse sleeps in a bed too small for him. Along the other, Rosalie's mattress is pushed. I can barely make out her crouched form in the semi-darkness, but I draw closer until I see how her stomach contracts and she holds it with both arms, her tiny hands clinging to her right ribcage like starfish. In front of her, the vivid yellow pool spreads and seeps into her mattress in a way that lets me know it's been there awhile and is probably cold.

"Da . . . ddy," she moans slow, her voice tight with pain. It sounds wrong in a child's voice.

"Hi there, sweetheart," I whisper so as not to scare her. "Your daddy will be right back. Do you need anything? Some water?" Reaching out, I softly scratch her back with my fingertips, and instantly feel the heat through her thin nightgown.

"Hurts so bad. Can't get up," she whispers through dry lips. "I want Daddy."

"He should be here any second." I glance over my shoulder to where the front door is in sight. "I'll stay with you till he gets here." As I run my fingers through her hair, she suddenly jerks, and I can see tear trails along her cheeks.

"Ahhh!" She crumbles into herself, pulling her knees nearly to her chin. *"Daddy!"* Her scream is raw, pure desperation. Something is *very wrong.* Ragged sobs shake her tiny frame. Her agony splits through my memories to when I was the little girl crying out in the dark. They say we can't feel another's pain, but this one I know.

"Rosa? What's wrong?" Jesse sits up in bed, eyes half open.

"Shhh, shh, it's okay. He's coming." I ignore the boy and try to soothe her trembling body.

"No!" She pushes me away with one arm, as if I were a complete stranger. "*Daddy!!*"

I stand, my heart sinking like a ship at sea. "I'll get him," I promise. "Hang on, I'll get him. Jesse." I turn to him. "You stay right with her. Don't leave her alone."

He nods, climbing from bed to stand at his sister's side.

Flying from the cabin, I spot Henry carrying the large pot of water, his eyes both light and clouds, like a sea storm passing. I run to him as I shout.

"Henry! It's Rosalie!"

The panic in my voice tells the rest.

He thrusts the water pot to the ground, most of it sloshing out and turning the dust to mud. In two strides, he is next to me, and we rush back in together.

In the tiny room, Jesse stands over his sister, eyes wide as if he'd just thrown a live grenade. "She's lots worse than last night." He looks up at his dad, his face begging for everything to be made better.

Henry stoops over his daughter, and immediately she turns and tucks into him, sobbing. Watching them, I know that nothing on this earth could compare to the security and comfort of being in her father's arms. I can't stop looking at them, at the way he almost absentmindedly brushes his lips across her forehead. What a terrible, beautiful moment. To need someone so completely, then to have that need met so fully. To be loved with abandon.

Again Rosalie's hands cling to her right ribcage, forcing my old childhood memory to the surface. "Henry," I speak up as I hunch behind him, but he doesn't seem to hear me. "Henry." I glide my hand down his arm, then fold my fingers into his. He blinks and brings his eyes to meet mine. "Look at this." I point. "Her appendix is here. Mine burst years ago—I'd bet that's what is happening."

He nods, the clouds in his eyes a snowstorm. "I have to go find Dr. Allred."

He attempts to stand, but Rosalie clings to him and cries out, "No! You have to stay!" A drowning cat would be calmer. Her thin arms claw at his shirt, refusing to let go.

"She should go with you," I urge. "The doctor must treat her immediately."

"There's no way she's well enough to travel." Henry shakes his head. "I'd have to go slow or she'd be in agony. No, I can ride as fast as possible and get the doctor to her in less time."

"You can't leave!" she sobs, her cry splitting the air, leaving it shattered and broken.

She needs him. She buries her face in his chest, and it seems that just to breathe his scent calms her. The rock of his body back and forth is a taste of medicine. I know what it's like to need help like that, but to go without the safety of strong arms.

But if I go, Warren will find me. I *know* it. Call it clairvoyance or an insight from the heavens, but somehow I am *certain* that I won't be lucky enough for Warren not to spot me. To walk out this door will be to walk into the lion's den. And when he finds me, the best-case scenario is that he drags me home for a sound beating and life under his thumb. The cursed life.

Worst case is that my body is found in the mountains, with no way for anyone to know what he had done. Both are completely within the realm of possibility.

It's the tiny girl's life, or my own. It's the security her father brings, or the destruction of mine.

Jesse reaches forward and places his hand on his sister's shoulder. The movement makes me look down, realizing I haven't pulled my hand from Henry's. His fingers grasp mine with the same intensity that his daughter clutches

him. The touch reminds me of birds, both soft and soothing, yet wild and earnest. Suddenly, crouched there in the
dim room, I become aware of a strange bond surging
between our touches like a current's flow. Our souls all
echo Rosalie's cries, to have someone to stay with us. In
this moment, we are both beggars and givers. Each of us
hurting, each of us helping. And I am part of this small
circle.

They've slipped past my walls. We huddle, our backs
against the ache of the world, together. Suddenly I feel a
love for them strong enough to break my heart. I love
them, every single one of them, like I've never loved
anyone before.

I love them more than my freedom.

That's it. I have to do this. For Rosalie, and for each of
them. For Henry.

"Stay with her. I'll go," The whisper escapes. Henry
unburies his face from his daughter's matted hair and
meets my eyes. "I'll be back." I should have told him my
father was in town, but now it's too late. All I can do is
give a small encouraging smile and pray I just spoke
the truth.

Rosalie moans, her sweet face pinching in pain, and
curls even tighter into herself.

"Thank you," Henry says so quietly, the words are
almost mouthed. Responding with only a nod, I let go of
his hand and step back from the circle. Yet the current
continues to flow through me, as cleansing and enlivening
as lying in a cool stream.

There's not a moment to lose. As I turn to run from the
room, suddenly Henry grasps at my arm. "Wait!" My gaze
falls to his hand, then follows it to his face. At those beautifully dark eyes, the tiny baby hairs on the back of my neck
rise, and for a moment they seem to tell me that he wants

me here, that it pains him to let me go just as much as it would Rosalie for him.

"Your horse is tired. Take mine. Rocinante is rested—he'll be much faster. He's in the barn."

But his hand stays on my arm, his touch strong and gentle at the same time. Forcing myself to find breath, I lock eyes with him. "It's going to be all right. Everything is going to be fine."

He nods, lifting his hand, and turns his attention fully back to the sick child sobbing in his arms.

Racing to the barn, I find his horse. Grabbing the reins but without bothering with a saddle, I climb onto him bareback. Lady whinnies as Henry's horse and I race past onto the mountain trail. The horse is fleet of foot and the wind from our speed chills me down to my bone marrow. Henry's horse.

Rocinante.

Don Quixote's horse.

All I can hope is that like Don Quixote, Rocinante and I can find the sheer willpower to conquer the giant before us.

Chapter Eleven

My knuckles rap hard on the doctor's door with a determination that probably tells him he is needed to either keep someone from leaving this life or to help someone enter it. He *has to* help. If he can't make Rosalie well, we have no other options. He is the answer that we must trust completely, the elixir that must be taken. Whether to heal or make worse, he holds our only hope.

As I raise my hand to knock the second time, the door opens, a woman with soft edges standing in the doorway. She points at me, "You're that girl staying with Alvin and Elleny, aren't you?"

"Please!" I clutch the frame without saying so much as a hello. "I need the doctor. It's a child. Her appendix—"

But the woman shakes her head and points toward Main Street, her eyes turned down at the corners. "He's just gone to the bank to apply for a loan—you'll find him there. Go!"

Spinning on my toes I race back to Rocinante, and we

bolt in the direction the woman pointed. She calls something after us, but I can't make it out.

As we turn onto the busy road, we alone move faster than a trot. Normally only children or thieves run, and as we ride by, we are as discreet as a lance. People part for us, and I can feel their gazes on my back after we go. Spotting the bank, I find a post to tie Rocinante to and dismount. Knotting the reins, I look up and see him.

My father.

Speaking with someone I do not know. Towering over the other man. With light brown hair combed to the side and crisp-tailored suit, he looks the perfect gentleman.

The simple knowledge that he is right before me settles over my skin, leaving my flesh prickly. I don't feel surprise. I knew he'd be here—somehow I did. He stands talking to a stranger not five feet from the doors I need to walk through to find the doctor. There is no way to avoid him seeing me unless I wait, which isn't an option for Rosalie's sake. I had been lucky enough to avoid him for days now—months, really. Perhaps I was just trapping myself by staying here, like chickens in a pen, thin wire separating them from the coyote. But does it matter how long I was lucky if the coyote only has to be lucky once?

Exhaling slowly, I try to urge my legs to move, but they stay stiff as rods. *I must do this*, I remind myself. *For Rosalie. For Henry.* The current I felt kneeling in the children's dark room hasn't left me, but now it seems like whitewater. Likely to bash my head into a rock, overpowering, something I can't begin to believe I could control. Love, it turns out, is as dangerous as I always believed it would be.

Taking a step back so Rocinante blocks me from view, my breath becomes haggard. A purple terror wraps its fingers around my throat.

When I was young, almost twelve years old, I had gone

to the village preacher for help. I told him that my father was hurting me, that I couldn't stop him. At first he didn't believe me—he didn't say it, but I could tell. Eventually I convinced him, but all the preacher did was sternly call Warren to repentance, then left Warren to take his shame out on me. I couldn't get out of bed for days afterward, and once, when Warren was gone, the preacher visited me. He was grieved, he said.

"I wish I could do more. But you are his daughter. What else can I do? Kidnap you?"

Yes, I had insisted. *Yes, yes, please.* But he just stood and walked away, closing the door on my childhood sobs. For hours afterwards, I wailed, spine curled into a ball, fingers twisting in the thin sheets on the bed.

I had never known until then what it felt like to be hopeless. Never before or ever since have I been so desperate. Until now.

How noble it felt to come here, when there was a beautiful quivering child an arm's reach away, her father's back arched protecting her just as I'd always wanted someone to treat me.

But that was before I actually had to face my father.

Now I stand all alone, hands trembling as I bring them to my lips. They are not here, and he is. If I step out from behind this horse and he sees me, everything that is good in my life will end. *He will kill me,* I think over and over. *He is going to kill me.* Even if he beats me and leaves me alive, he will not stop until he has killed my spirit. I will never set foot in those mountains again, never know the feel of Lady's smooth back as we glide, perhaps never even be allowed to caress the pages of a book again.

I'll never again see the very people I gave all that up for, as long as I live.

Closing my eyes, I try to see their faces. Jesse's blue

eyes, the exact shade as the sky above their fields as he plowed behind the horse much too big for him.

Rosalie, curls bouncing, always loving without restraint, happier to see me than anyone in my life.

And Henry. His hands holding my own, our palms held against each other as if in a soft kiss, showing me that a man who is gentle is the strongest of men, and a truly strong man is gentle. Thinking of them, the current swells again over me, and my breath becomes even. If I could choose any family on earth, they are the one I would want.

The love extends beyond boundaries until even the portrait on the wall comes to mind and I feel love for her. Their mother, the woman Henry loved and grieved. I love her for creating this family, and as I think of her, I realize a kinship. She and I both know what it is to love these precious people, and have to face leaving them. I can't think of anything harder to consider.

But, she seems to whisper, and I almost can feel her next to me, holding the baby she gave her life for. *We all give our lives up to something. There is nothing better to give yourself for than the chance to sacrifice yourself for those you love. Some of us are simply called to give more than others.* Like the sun loves the moon, it must willingly sink into night so that the other may shine.

I open my eyes and lean forward until Warren comes into sight. The stranger speaking to him gestures widely as he speaks, clearly settled into conversation. But then through the bank windows, I see a figure I recognize. The doctor sits, back stooped over one side of a desk, confirming what his wife said. I have to go to him, and too much time has been wasted already.

Securing the reins, I run a hand down Rocinante's face, steadying myself. *Rocinante.* The name brings to mind so many from literature who gave themselves for love, for the highest call. Yet, this time I don't pretend to be any of them. This is *my* journey. Stepping from these shadows, I face my past. My past of having the wind knocked from me, of nursing my own wounds, butterfly bandaging my cut lips in pale lamp light as my entire body aches. It is not Buck or Dorothy or Don Quixote, but I who will give up a future as beautiful and brilliantly bright as the sun.

With a final deep breath, I step from the shadow of the horse.

Warren doesn't turn, and I pick up my pace.

Breaking into a run, I come closer and closer until I can see every detail in his stance, all of it familiar to me. The stranger looks up at the woman careening toward them, and I can see Warren's face slightly turn to see what the man is staring at. Before he can turn, I am there, for an instant our arms almost brushing, then as a fast as if the devil himself were after me, I dash past him and through the glass door of the bank.

The doctor sits at the desk, nodding as the banker points to paperwork in front of them.

"Dr. Allred!" I nearly collide into the desk. "Rosalie Sterling—her appendix. She can't be moved." I gasp for breath, but he's heard all he needs to know.

Standing, he nods to the banker. "I must go. Please hold on to these and we will resume this as soon as possible." The banker nods, and the doctor turns to me. "I know where they live. Let's go."

He begins to march toward the door, but all I see is Warren on the other side of the glass, his lips set thin and straight as a blade. His eyes meet mine, boiling with hatred, a satisfaction in his eyes as he knows the noose is tightening around my neck. I can't get away. Frantically, I look around the bank for a back door, but see none available. If there is one, it's probably tucked out of sight to complicate esape for robbers.

Perhaps if I'm not alone, he won't risk the public attention. In two quick bounds, I'm next to the doctor, close as cold is to ice. He jerks slightly to the side, no doubt surprised at my audacity in invading his personal space as we step through the glass door as one.

Where Warren waits.

My heart batters my ribcage, a cornered animal, as I cling to the doctor's side and keep my chin up but my gaze away from Warren. He can see how my chest heaves with each breath like a terrified rabbit, but I try set my face to appear calm.

One step. Two. Dr. Allred is between me and Warren as we stride around him. The doctor is speaking, but dread bellows so loudly in my ears, I can't hear anything else. We pass Warren, but I know he's there, following.

Suddenly, the doctor stops at a pure black stallion and quickly mounts. "Meet you there." He nods down at me and takes off, leaving me alone and vulnerable on the sidewalk.

Fingers grip my forearm, strong enough to bruise. My father yanks hard, spinning me into him until he clasps my other arm and his face is only inches from mine. I squirm, but he only thinly smiles and grasps me the harder. The message is clear—to struggle will only tighten the knot around my neck. He knows I'm not strong enough to fight back alone.

Alone.

I am not alone.

"Scoundrel!" I scream as loud as I can. "Pervert!" On the crowded street, I feel a shift as every neck cranes to see what the yelling is about. From that preacher as a child, I learned not to put anyone who would help me in a compromised position. No one wants to tangle in father-daughter warfare—they'd be unsure who to believe. And certainly no one desires to take on a seriously dangerous stranger. I need to make this as uncomplicated as possible for them. "Don't you *dare* touch me like that, you sick old man! Let me go!" My spittle lands on Warren's face, his jaw clenching and unclenching.

"*Enough.*" He barely moves his mouth. "You are coming with me. Shut your mouth or I swear, oh, I promise you, Marian, I *will* kill you."

But I'd heard that snake hiss those words in my mind so much over the months that now that they've been said, the shock has worn off. *Of course you'll kill me. No matter what I do. So what's to stop me?*

"Someone! Get him, please!" I plead to the crowd. All eyes are on us.

No, wait—they're not. Everyone watches us, concern etched in the corners of their eyes, but now and then, their glances scan the crowd. Watching to see who will step forward.

They know what's right. They even *want to do it*—I see it on their faces. But there's dozens of people here, so who does the responsibility fall to? It's diluted among them all. They could stand there and watch him beat me until my blood flows on the street, and though they'd go home with some shame, it would only be a piece, a tiny part. They'd say to themselves, "What could I have done?" And their consciences would be pacified, as they told themselves they were just going home, just coming from work, and they shouldn't have been there anyway.

But they are. What they are seeing can't be unseen. One can't simply be a bystander—it carries with you and evolves until you forever have to live with being a witness.

"You two!" I jerk my head at two capable-looking men

93

nearby. "And you and you!" I lock eyes with each one and they know—*the weight is now on you.*

Everyone on the street leans around each other, trying to get a look at the four men I singled out.

"You're *done*," Warren hisses in my ear and tries to pull me down the street.

"Stop!" One of the men, a red-haired fellow with more freckles than I've seen in my life, calls out. Jerking away from Warren, I see the four men all look at each other and then slowly—much too slowly for my preference—nod and step forward. That step forward was all they needed for their feet and minds to become set. Their speed increases until they each are barreling at Warren. Brows furrowed, jaws harden, and I think they must see their own daughters and wives in my place.

"*Back off!!*" Warren releases one of my arms, still clutching tightly to the other. His free hand whips to his belt and pulls out a knife, its steel glinting in the sunlight.

My bravado flees. No one is going to risk a blade in the gut, not when they have a family waiting at home. Fear puts a palm over my mouth and pinches my nose, suffocating me. This is it—Warren really is going to take me. Three of the men tense and slow as Warren takes a step backwards, his grip on my arm a tourniquet.

Until the freckled fellow just tips his head as if to say, *Well, then, if it comes to that.* And he pulls a gun from his own side.

Hallelujah that we live in backcountry Kentucky rather than pacifist Oregon is all I can say. This never would have happened there.

At last, Warren's fingers release me, and he slowly raises his two hands above his head. "This is ridiculous. That's my *daughter.*" The crowd becomes all tittering whispers and questioning looks, but I just lift my eyebrows and scoff.

"You should hope not! That would make what you did all the more disgusting!" I step away from him toward my protectors. Touching two of them on the arms, I smile, relief flowing through me as light does through sunset clouds. "I can't thank you enough."

They nod back, and the redhead speaks for the group. "Glad you're safe now, ma'am. Someone—you there. Find an officer and let's see what we are going to do about this guy."

"Yeah." Warren nods, the vein in his neck pulsing. "Get an officer here. We'll let him decide who is telling the truth."

A police officer? I hadn't thought this through that far. What will come from all this if we are both questioned? They'll find out that there are no witnesses to molestation, and he actually *is* my father. And since it has been months since I ran away, there is no proof of the cruelty he has done to me— the bruises have faded away, the burned skin has healed. All I have is old scars that could be from anything, and my word. A word that dozens will quickly discredit as belonging to a liar.

Whatever judgments a police officer may pass, it certainly wouldn't get me back to Rosalie's side quickly, and could easily have me left in my *dear* old father's care, having no husband to claim me.

"You'll excuse me, gentlemen." I step back. "But there's a child I must see to."

"Wha. . .?" One of the other four men speaks up. "Where are you going? You can't go now."

"I must," is all I answer with a quick nod. Then, leaving them scratching their beards and looking at each other unsure, I run back to Rocinante.

"Hey, that's *Henry Sterling's* horse -" One man's voice cuts in from behind me.

I cringe. If I tell them Henry let me use it, it will confirm to Warren exactly where to go. Already too much has been said. Pretending not to hear, I pull myself onto the horse's bare back.

"Only *thieves* ride bareback," Warren's voice shouts over my shoulder, and I know he's getting less scared of that silver gun by the minute. "She *stole* my horse. Maybe you people have seen it? A mare, brown?"

"Oh, yes," another voice speaks up, and though I don't look, I think it might just be that vinegar-lipped woman whose job I took those many weeks ago. "I've seen her riding a horse like that all over the mountain!"

"Yah!" I kick Rocinante and we take off. Not toward the mountain.

My stomach wants to climb up my throat as I turn my back away from the direction of the cabin on the hill. There's nowhere on earth I would rather be than by Rosalie's side right now, Henry's calm steadiness assuring all of us that everything is going to be okay. But if I go there, Warren will follow. Right now I know his gaze is on my back, watching, wondering, "*Where is she running to?*" and wherever I go, he will ask around who has seen me. If I go to Henry, Rosalie, and Jesse, I'll be leading a wolf straight to the pen.

This is it. I have to run.

Chapter Twelve

A tear streaks straight back from the corner of my eye as Rocinante rides fast. I don't care where we are going—any direction at all that won't lead Warren straight to Henry's cabin. Above me, the sky's moody and the afternoon is heavy with clouds, the color of lost hopes. The air feels too thick and I gasp, chest heaving, for breath.

I have to go. *Now.*

By staying this long, I've only set fire to the bridge I was standing on. My heart feels gouged, as surely as if a dagger were trying to stop its beating. How can a person go on living with this much pain coursing through them? It would have been better if I'd never stayed in this town. If I'd never met Henry and his beautiful children.

I've said so many goodbyes. I said it as a child as when I sat at the front room window, waiting for a mother who would never return. I said it then, my breath fogging up the glass, not comprehending one iota what it meant. Later I said it without a word, without a glance behind me. I've said goodbye with a dance in my heart. I've said it just to end up being wrong, to turn around and come back. But I've never had to face a goodbye like this. Like it would be easier to carve my heart from my chest and leave it in their hands, then go forward and actually believe I could live without it. I hate this goodbye the most of any I've ever had to give, and still, more than anything, I wish I could actually have the chance to say those tiny words.

That I could actually see those sweet faces one last time.

Maybe I can. The thought toys with me.

No, no, it's too dangerous, I argue with myself. I feel soft and weak from hunger. My sleepless nights are catching up to me, and I can't seem to make my zig-zagging thoughts go in a straight line. *Think, think!*

Warren *should be* occupied at the police station for a while. That will surely buy me an hour at least.

And what about Rocinante? I can't just steal him. Leaving Lady is hardly a fair trade—she's much older and can't haul the loads around the farm that Rocinante can. Besides, Lady has been my dearest friend on this journey. Must I say goodbye to her as well?

Pulling the reins up, I bring Rocinante to a trot. *Okay, breath, think clearly.* Warren will be with the police for a while, and even if he is released, the townspeople are now suspicious of him. It's a small town—by the end of the day, most everyone will have heard about our encounter. He can't so easily ask around about me now, no matter what the police decide. I don't have to be quite so frantic.

Perhaps I could go get my few belongings from Alvin and Elleny's, thank them for their kindness, then return the horse to Henry and say my goodbyes. If my father follows my trail, they can tell him I'm gone, that he won't find me there. He wouldn't waste time harming them if he knows I'm getting farther away by the minute.

Yes. I can be bait. Lead him away from the people I've come to care about. This could work.

Rocinante comes to a stop at my yank on the reins.

"Come on, boy. I need your help just a bit more."

Tying Rocinante to the tree outside the barn, I yell out, "Elleny? Alvin?" Their Buick is gone, but I spare just a few seconds to run to the door of the house and pound on it. "Are you home??"

No answer, and my heart sinks. My fingers lightly touch the door, and words come out in a whisper. "You've been so good to me."

But there isn't time for pause. Racing back to the barn, I climb up into the loft. Though I can tell where Elleny came to retrieve clothes for the daily bundle they have left me, most everything else goes untouched. The quilt is still turned down—the new pair of britches and blouse are draped across the end of the bed. Though most other Pack Horse Librarians wear them for convenience' sake, I had hesitated because Elleny expressed opinions about how audaciously unladylike they are. Eventually, after about the hundred and thirtieth time of having my dress be a nuisance, I made up my mind to buy a pair. It came as no surprise that she never packed them in my bundle. Now, however, I snatch them up and begin changing. Perhaps if I can find a hat to hide my hair, I can pass for a man at a distance, enough to fool Warren at least.

On the bedside crate, my remaining books still sit, *Don Quixote* propped open. Fingers finishing my last button, I reach down and pull the books to my chest. Scanning the loft, I search for some way to carry them, my pack still being at Henry's. Walking to my shallow clothes crate, I pull out a long-sleeved dress and spread it out on the bed. Then I empty the crate onto the skirt and set the books on top.

Opening *The Wizard of Oz,* I flip to the title page and rip it out. I've never intentionally harmed any book before —they have been my children that I carefully tucked in from the cold and wet. I wonder if Alvin and Elleny will know that when they see the page, if they'll understand what words aren't enough to say. A pencil sits on the crate, and I lean over to scrawl my note carefully on the page where the crate's old slats hold strong.

> *Alvin & El,*
>> *Thank you for loving me as if I were your own.*
>> *Goodbye, and God bless.*
>> *M*

Then leaving the note, I turn and tuck the skirt ends around my small pile of clothes and books into a bundle, tying it off with the sleeves. I slip my arm through the knot, and it sits in the crook of my elbow. I step back and spare a single moment to look at the tiny loft. The only place I ever truly felt was home.

As I ride to the cabin, the air has turned sore and the sky is full of bruises, black and deep blue. Rocinante's speed is like nothing Lady has ever done, and I crouch close to his neck not to fall off. The cabin comes into view, and my heart feels torn down its seams at the sight.

Enduring my father's anger all my life was horrible. A childhood abandoned by my mother was brutal. Running away and making my own way in the world with nothing to my name took me low, so low. But each of those times, I had felt an unconquerable something still beating in my chest. I believed there could be better days ahead.

Yet now I can't fathom that anything coming can compare to what I could have had in those sturdy walls. I fooled myself into believing that could be my world, but it's as impossible as finding Oz over a rainbow, as delusional as believing a windmill is a giant.

There's no corner of their universe I hadn't hoped to share. I realize now that when I saw Jesse struggling in the field behind a horse that was much too big for him, I also saw myself coming to the boy, bracing myself behind him, easing his burden.

When Rosalie tucked into her father's chest as she hurt down to her very core, I nearly felt the small head cradled against my own bosom, and imagined what it would be like to brush a kiss almost absent-mindedly across her forehead. For her to find comfort in *my* arms, to call *my* name out in the night.

And Henry. Every inch of that home could have held a little moment that will now never be. Would he have brought me a wildflower when he came in for lunch, and I'd turn and place it in the Mason jar on the windowsill with the others? While I cooked bacon and toast, would he have flipped the eggs, the kids running into the tiny kitchen and begging like chicks? When the nights were cold, would he have gotten up in the dark and fetched an extra blanket, tucking it around me before getting in as well and huddling close for more than just warmth? Thinking of it, my chin quivers as I try hopelessly to control my emotion. Tears blind my eyes, but the horse knows his way.

As the years pass, will Henry still take my memory and examine it as he starts his day, as he did his wife's portrait? Did I mean that much to him? For I know he did to me.

This is what I could have found in that tiny home. The chance to love and be loved without any restraint. A fool's dream. A torture from my own imagination. This loving and leaving is the most painful thing I have ever had to endure, for it rips to my very core until even my soul is filleted open, gaping and raw.

I will never do this to myself again. I can never let myself love like this, not even once more, as long as I live.

Drops begin to fall lightly from the sky as Rocinante and I reach Henry's home. I hear the scream before I even reach the door, just undiluted terror. A child's voice should never have to sound like that.

Lady is still tied to a tree near the house, and I secure Rocinante's reins to another nearby. Knowing that Henry and Jesse have more important worries than answering the door, I slow my steps and then walk in without knocking.

The child now lays on a couple of thin blankets spread across the kitchen table, thrashing and sobbing. The doctor, along with her father and brother, huddle around her like cats, but if they try to touch her, she pushes them all away. At the sound of the door closing, Henry looks up and locks eyes with mine.

Crossing the room in a few wide steps, he wraps his arms around me, back arched, and tucks his face down until his cheek rests against my head. He seems so ready to collapse from worry that I wonder if I could hold his dead weight. My heart picks up pace to have him so close, to be the one he is finding some solace in.

"Thank you." His voice sounds hoarse. "I can't bear to think that without a doctor——" He chokes on his words and stops.

"What's happening?" I ask, peering around him.

"We explained that she needs surgery and must be sedated. Then she went completely mad." Henry gestures to his daughter. His face looks as though he's sinking in quicksand. "The doctor can't administer the drug with her like this. She *has to* calm down."

An idea hits me, and I drop my arms from around Henry. Tugging at the bundle I packed, I set it on a chair nearby and it falls open. There on top, as though waiting, is *The Wizard of Oz*.

Thumbing through it, I know exactly which pages I'm looking for. With my fingers sticking in to save my places, I hold it to my chest and sprint to Rosalie's side. I open the book and start to read aloud over the girl's wails.

"'The cyclone had set the house down gently, very gently—for a cyclone—in the midst of a country of marvelous beauty. There were lovely patches of green sward all about, with stately trees bearing rich and luscious fruits. Banks of gorgeous flowers were on every hand, and birds with rare and brilliant plumage sang and fluttered in the trees and bushes.'" Rosalie still writhes, but her sobs have turned a few decibels down, and I know she's listening. "'A little way off was a small brook, rushing and sparkling along between green banks, and murmuring in a voice very grateful to a little girl who had lived so long on the dry, gray prairies.'" With that I give Rosalie a knowing look, as if she were the very girl the book spoke of. Her shoulders shudder with sobs, her eyes bloodshot from crying, but she looks at me.

Crouching, I kneel beside the table so I can look the dear child right in the face. "Have you ever heard this story, *The Wizard of Oz?*"

She shakes her head as a trembling breath escapes.

"Oh, you'd *love* it. A tornado picks this girl and her dog up from their farm and takes her to the most wonderful place. She meets tiny people—munchkins, they are called—and all sorts of other amazing creatures. A tinman, a scarecrow, witches, and a wizard. One of her dearest friends the cowardly lion. Have you ever heard of something so silly?? A lion who is afraid of everything!"

She doesn't smile, as though she is quite decided to stay

miserable, but her gaze stays on my face. On either side, I can feel the others watching, silent.

"'But that isn't right.'" I try on a new voice as I find my next page, not caring if I look ridiculous to the others. "'The King of Beasts shouldn't be a coward,' said the Scarecrow.

"'I know it,' returned the Lion, wiping a tear from his eye with the tip of his tail. 'It is my great sorrow, and makes my life very unhappy. But whenever there is danger, my heart begins to beat fast.'

"'Perhaps you have heart disease,' said the Tin Woodman.

"'It may be,' said the Lion.'" I stop and squint at the girl. "Heart disease! Nonsense. I don't think they understood very much what it takes to be brave. Listen to this." I flip one more time, now toward the end of the book. "'You have plenty of courage, I am sure,' answered the wizard. 'All you need is confidence in yourself. *There is no living thing that is not afraid when it faces danger.*'" Pausing, I meet Rosalie's eyes before continuing. Her breath comes out slow and heavy, yet the rest of her now lies still except for a bead of sweat that streaks a trail down her forehead. Reaching up, I take her hand in mine, then read on. "'The *true courage* is in facing danger when you *are* afraid, and *that* kind of courage you have in *plenty.*'" Giving her hand a squeeze, I smile at her. "I know you do." She looks down for a moment, and I realize her gaze has fallen to the book.

For just a moment, I look at it too, and know what I should do.

It's just one more goodbye. And right now, though I love these bound pages as fiercely as I ever did, they seem to matter less. Someone else needs to find the wizard now. Letting go of Rosalie's hand, I place the book in it instead. "I want you to have this." The girl's eyes widen, and she looks at me as if I'd just materialized from a bubble. Her fingers curl over it, and without a word, she slides it across the table to her heaving chest.

"You're going to go to sleep now." I brush a dark curl from Rosalie's forehead and smile at her. "And when you dream, perhaps you will visit Oz. Say hello to the munchkins for me." I lean forward and kiss the child on the forehead. "I love you, Rosalie," I whisper. The first person I've said those words to as far back as I can remember. "I really do." A tear slides down my cheek and rests in the corner of my lips. I lick it, and it tastes of salt. I'll always remember that as what love tastes like.

"I love you too," she whispers, and my grief washes over me, leaving my strength sapped.

Standing, the doctor doesn't miss his cue. I don't look at him, though. Instead, my eyes stay locked with Rosalie's as he begins to administer the sedative. She stiffens at his touch, but doesn't scream—just holds the book so tightly, her little knuckles turn white.

"There will be a beautiful good witch you will meet, all pink and ruffles. Deep breaths, my dear—deep, deep breaths." I keep talking just to get her mind off the doctor. "There are flowers as big as your face, and the most remarkable Emerald City, where the wizard is waiting for you."

Her eyelids flutter.

"And don't worry—as amazing at it is, I know you'll find your way home. When you wake up, your father and Jesse will be right here." Her eyes close, and I reach forward and place my hands on hers as they finally relax around my old worn book. I used to think there was nothing I could love more than my books.

Her dark eyelashes fall still against her soft cheeks, her curls spread about her head like a halo, and I think she must be the most beautiful thing I've ever seen. "'There's no place like home,'" I whisper, my goodbye balling up in my chest.

Stepping back, I turn to the chair where my belongings lay, and I tie up the corners before anyone can notice how weak my knees have become, how my hands tremble.

"Marian."

Looking up, I see that Henry's face is soft, his gaze like flowing water that would sweep me away. His dark eyes meet mine, and he steps forward as though to take me in his arms again. If anything could make this farewell more painful than it already is, it is that.

I can't do it. I can't set the goodbye free. It stays trapped inside me as I look at Henry.

Dropping his gaze, I turn without a word and open the door, then run out into the rain where Lady waits.

Chapter Thirteen

The rain falling from the graphite sky carries the chill of autumn and the scent of sunburnt leaves. Though it isn't falling hard, it's been going a while now, and both horses are as drenched as if they'd gone for a swim. Rain and tears mingle on my cheeks, and my stomach churns like a black water eddy, all the love and grief inside me with nowhere to go, just spinning around and around.

Reaching Lady, I slip the bundle I carry onto a fence post then pry my fingers at her tied reins, but Henry's unfamiliar knot and the tears blinding my vision leave my hands fumbling helplessly. Behind me, I hear the door open and heavy steps on the cabin steps.

"Marian! What? Where are you going?"

I shake my head, not trusting my voice, but then Henry is here, his hand on my arm, as if he knows his touch alone could have the strength to stop me.

But I can't let it.

Meeting his eyes, the words come in a whisper. "My father. He's here, in town. He's coming."

For a moment, Henry digests this, then nods, the solution clear to him. "I'll protect you. I won't let him touch you. You have my word."

"No." I shake his hand from my arm and dig my fingers into the snarl of reins. "You don't understand. If he follows me away from here, he will leave your family alone, but if he finds me with you—"

The reins come loose finally, but Henry reaches over and holds Lady by the noseband. "We have three grown adults here right now—he's outnumbered. You don't have to go."

"He'll be back. As long as he knows I'm close, your family won't be safe." I try to remove his hand from Lady's flash, but Henry doesn't loosen his grip. "You have to think of your children!" I insist.

With his other hand, Henry reaches up and rests his fingers along my cheekbone. "I am," he whispers over the rain. "We need you." He leans close, closer than he has ever been before, and I ache to fold into him, for every solid piece of him to wrap around every soft curve of mine. "I need you." With a step, his body is against my own, and his lips whisper against the corner of my lips. "Stay. Please stay." His plea comes out so soft, yet with the power to nearly bring me to my knees. He must have dropped his hand from Lady, for his fingers find my waist and pull me close.

I don't answer, and his lips brush my against mine, the sweetest touch I've known. Closing my eyes, I feel his every touch like sunshine, impossibly gentle until it's almost painful. I open my mouth to tell him I must go, but only a whimper comes out.

"I love you," he whispers the moment before his lips fall upon mine, tasting like shooting stars and angel dust.

His kiss upends me, and softly he groans as if waiting to do this was a great effort he can at last put down.

How is this happening? Every inch of him is pressed against me, begging me to stay, with taut muscles and sturdy hands that are much more convincing than words. *He* loves *me*. He loves me and *I love him*.

His lips leave mine, but he hovers close, in a place we have created with our own breath.

"I love you too," I whisper. But then slowly, I open my eyes.

After days without rest, facing my father, and leaving Rosalie, my strength should be completely drained to nothing. But like a well fills with water, I find just enough from somewhere deep inside me. I take two steps back until his hands fall from my waist. "Don't think that my leaving means I love you less." Meeting his sweet, dark eyes, there seems a pulse between us, a heartbeat from the earth or the rain or each other. "It means I love you more. More than I ever knew I could."

Standing there in the rain that would smudge the earth around us like a Van Gogh painting, our locked gazes see into each other's souls. I think for a moment that he knows my fears—he understands that just because this is something I have to do, that doesn't make it any easier. Ever so slowly, at the pace of a beautiful sunset ending, Henry nods. Not because he agrees, but because he knows that he can no sooner control me than push back winter.

"I can't make you stay," he says. "But I don't believe you're leaving just because of your father."

"Of course that's why I have to go. You're all in danger if I stay."

He shakes his head. "Marian, I have a hunting rifle in there. I'm a grown man, not a child. It's my *responsibility* to protect the people I love."

"And what? You'll never sleep? You'll patrol every inch of your land, always stay right by our sides?"

"I'm not saying he isn't a threat." Henry exhales slowly. "I'm saying that even though you stayed in town and found a job, you haven't stopped running since that night I met you in the woods. You have so much love to give—I see it in how you taught Rosalie to read, and in how you gave Jesse your most prized possession. Your playfulness and silly accents show it! How could I *not* fall for you? But as soon as anyone wants to get close to you, you put up walls."

Without meaning to, his words smack, and I lurch back. Is he right? Is this about more than just Warren? I have kept my love under lock and key, taking it out here and there to show the children how prettily it shines, but then quickly tucking it away again. Where nothing bad can happen.

"The walls keep me safe," I whisper. "Look at this." I blink, then gesture at the cabin, "Look at this! Your daughter would have died if a doctor didn't get here in time! You love her so much, but then she'd be gone. It would have *killed* you. If life has taught me anything, it's that love *equals* pain. It's better not to care. Keep your heart safe." My shoulders sag as though I've been pulled up by my roots. "I do love you, Henry, you and your beautiful children. But it's destroying me. I can never let myself love like this again."

Henry steps forward and his hands find my arms, then he rubs them up and down them until I force myself to look up and meet his gaze.

"I know a thing or two about loss. And if *I've* learned anything about life, it's that love is what puts fuel on your fire. It's what makes you get up every day and do what you do, and be willing to do it for the rest of your life. Marian, you tell yourself love is pain. That you can never let anyone in again. *No.* It's not *the love* that's destroying you. Don't you get it? It's your walls."

I don't answer. Something fiercer than love burns in my heart, something that tells me this is one of those moments when you question everything you know about life. That truth might not be so easily captured, but instead is a goldfish in a murky pool. Just when you think you've caught it, it slips through your fingers and leaves you back in an empty dark. For how else can one of the truths I knew be in such direct opposition to a truth Henry knows?

But even if Henry is right, what he suggests is not simple. Walls don't just crumble on demand. Brick by brick, I've built this room around myself, never knowing whether to fear most that it would be breached, or that it wouldn't.

"I want you to have something." I turn from him to the post where my bundle is tied. Carefully, I unknot it just enough to slip my last book out, and I hold it close to my chest, to protect it from the rain, I tell myself.

As I face Henry, the book feels almost warm in my fingers, almost like it has breath of its own. All the love of years are condensed in its pages. All the love I never got as a child, all the love I couldn't give settled here. To something that, for as alive as I'd make it out to be, could never love me back.

All that love bound tight, with nowhere to go. Until now. Until I finally let myself give it away. *Let myself*—what a simple thing to say, as if it were easy. Love is supposed to flow. And I suppose it does. Like blood. But at least it proves I'm alive.

"Your father's story." I hold it out to him as raindrops hit the cover like punctuation, like an ending.

But Henry doesn't reach out for it.

"Quick, it's getting wet!" I push it against his abdomen, yet he doesn't lift his hands.

"I can't." He looks away, but not so soon that I don't see tears brimming in his eyes. "It's your way of saying goodbye, but I can't."

We stand there, drenched in silence, both knowing I can't stay and he can't come with me. But still, what we must do feels impossible. To let go.

With a step forward, the worn book alone is between us as I lift my chin and bring my lips to his. The kiss tastes of the goodbye we cannot say, feather-light and sweet, gone too soon.

Pulling back, I look into those deep eyes of his. "Take it," I whisper. "Have something to remember me by."

Slowly, he raises his hands, and I feel the weight of the book lifted from my fingers.

His nostrils flare in and out to control his emotion, but he doesn't take his gaze from me as I turn and clasp the small bundle. Slipping it again into the crook of my arm, I brush a hand along Lady's backside, and then mount.

"If you ever decide to stop running, we'll be here." He looks up at me like a person buried in rubble looks toward a speck of light. Except how could I ever hope to save him when I feel pinned down by my own stones? They sit heavy on my chest, making each forced breath painful.

It's time to say what I must. I know it is. With a gentle touch, I open the cage inside me and set the words free.

"Goodbye, Henry," I whisper, chin shaking. "I'll love you as long as I live."

Kicking Lady's sides, I jerk forward and rush past the lovely cabin. I strain my eyes to see the children through the window, but all I can make out are the jars of wild-flowers on the sill. Lady and I push through Henry's land,

and it's only when we reach the tree line that I pull on the reins to stop.

Looking back, I see the home I almost had one last time. Birch and ancient pines reach their arms around the cabin, as if trying to shield it from the rest of the world.

If only that could be enough.

Under the evergreen's armor, Henry hasn't moved. The space between us feels charged, as if the very swaying wheat of his fields would speak to me. *Stay, stay,* the stalks whisper as they bend under the rainfall.

How I wish I could. That's my whole world over there. But instead, I stand on the edge and urge my horse to take a step.

With a click of my tongue to Lady, we disappear into the trees.

Chapter Fourteen

✦✦✦

My body racks with sobs as Lady climbs the mountainside. The adrenaline from the morning's events could only keep the physical toll of the last several days at bay for so long. But like a dark wave cresting, what was a distant roar now breaks over me. My soul itself is weary in a way that a good night's rest couldn't begin to fix.

All I wish is to turn around.

Without the hope of seeing their faces again, I am losing the desire for anything, any ambition, even my freedom. Despite my hunger, food holds no appeal. I have no taste for whatever life would offer. This day feels like being trapped in a nightmare, an imaginary day, that for some unexplainable reason I can't wake up from. Instead, the minutes trap me here, stretching into hours and then days and then a new life.

Tears cloud my vision, but even if I'd had my senses at full capacity, I doubt I would have seen Warren sooner.

As I round the corner, I see that he waits, his horse

blocking us from going any farther. Yanking on Lady's reins, I try to halt, but we are going too fast and almost collide with Warren.

All he has to do is reach over and his long fingers clasp through my hair. With a swift yank, he pulls me off Lady's back to the ground, my full body weight landing on my forearm. Grit and pebbles imbed in the skin, but I can't let a little dirt stop me. This is it. He's here to kill me.

Looking up, I see that to my right is a steep rock slope, and scrambling on all fours, I lunge up it. The sharp stones are difficult to grasp, cutting at my hands and knees, and the adrenaline I'd known earlier is nearly depleted. My breaths come out heavy, almost as if to weigh me down, as I scramble up the slick rock face.

"Did you think I *wouldn't* find you?" Warren's voice is ice cold, sending a shiver crawling down my spine and raising the hairs on my arms. "Did you actually think you could *hide?* I know you better than you know yourself, Marian. You're *predictable*. Nothing makes it easier to hunt something down." He tries to force his horse, Bolo, to follow, but the mud and slates of rock are too much on the steep hill. Bolo protests, shaking her mane, her eyes wild as the storm.

It's maybe thirty feet before the rock slope comes to a landing, and my fingers reach for the base of a small birch tree. Then I use it to heave myself over the lip of the ledge. Looking down, I see my father throw his leg over and begin to dismount, but a crack of thunder in the distance startles the horses. Lady stays put with her eyes fixed on me, but Bolo backs up at just the wrong moment, catching Warren's boot in the stirrup.

He stumbles as he lands, a curse on his lips for the animal, but it's only a second before he's back on his feet.

Bolo whinnies and stomps the wet ground, eyes wide to the storm crackling around her. And I realize, *Bolo has always spooked easily.* I can use that . . .

Warren crouches, climbing the steep rock slide after me. His lips are pinched thin—actually, all of him is thinner than ever before. He doesn't seem the bear of a man I always remembered him to be.

My legs quiver, and I cling to the birch to steady me, but it too trembles. I don't have the strength to outrun him, but here I do have higher ground. My mind attempts to grasp at a plan, but it's like trying to hold smoke in my hands, dissipating to nothing in my fingers. I strive to think clearly, but I have trouble even finding the *urge* to fight back. I've already given up everything I cared for most. Why can't he just let me rest? Why can't he just set me free, to live my life?

But no. That won't happen. If I'm going to find rest in this life, it's only going to be if I fight for it.

Near my feet is a large stone, and stooping, I pick it up and then raise it high. For the fraction of a moment, I pause, then with a short exhale, I chuck it straight down at Warren's head.

It slams directly into his collarbone, and he reels back. "Aww! You stupid—" But I don't stop to listen.

I start throwing or shoving every stone I can reach down the steep slope. He dodges the rest, but it forces him back down the hillside. His eyes glare at me, snake eyes, thin and intent, and his movements are jerky, favoring the broken collarbone piercing up at an odd angle. He's in pain, and all the more furious for it. But, I realize, he *is* weakened.

As with all evil, my attempts *do* keep him at bay, but if I ever stop fighting, he'll be upon me in seconds. There are only so many stones on this mountainside. I have to figure out what else to do.

Lightning cracks somewhere nearby, and the horses bellow in fear. But Bolo shakes her large head and stomps as though a demon has seized her.

"Thought you'd settle down, did you?" Warren taunts from the bottom of the rock slide. "Adopt that little family for your own, huh? Let me tell you, Marian—you never should have stopped here. You stupid, selfish girl. Only thinking of yourself. When I get you on this horse, you'll see what happens to anyone who tries to help you. The whole mountainside will see poor Henry's Sterling's cabin catch fire. 'The lightning struck so fast, they couldn't get out in time,' they'll say. They won't know what happened. But *you'll* know. You'll know what your selfishness has done to them."

For a moment, my world slows its spin as I stare down at that man I knew as my father. A green determination enters my bloodstream, my jaw becomes set, and my limbs stop shaking. All of a sudden, I think of Don Quixote facing his giants. To him those giants were *real*, a whole field of them standing in his way. But he didn't seem them as they really were.

Warren stands in my way, but suddenly I think I seem him as he really is. Hungry from weeks of living off the land chasing me, desperate to get the power back in his life, wounded and weakened in more ways than my stone could have done. He's not such a giant after all.

"You. Will. *Not.* Touch. Them." Each word comes out through clenched teeth as my spine straightens. Instead of answering, he draws his knife and comes at me again. Looking around, I try to find something to throw, but nothing that could stop him is within reach. I'm trapped up here.

My eyes scan the scene from this vantage point. Here I can see that the rock face is rectangular, with Warren coming up roughly the center. But if I scurry across this ridge to the left, there may be another path down. It would be steep, but if I can descend safely, it would bring me just a dozen feet behind my horse. Then if I can scare away Bolo so Warren can't follow, I can get to Lady. Perhaps I *can* escape. Lady meets my eyes and I think the horse understands my thoughts, bids me to come. Scuttling across the ledge, I come to the steep muddy path, scraggly bushes growing from the mountainside.

"Don't even think of it! The more you run, the worse it will be when I catch you!" Warren tries maneuvering to block my way, but the rock face is slick with few hand-holds. He can go up or down, but not to the side to block me.

Turning my stomach to the mountainside, I twist my hands around a handful of thin branches, and leaning back, I rappel the first several feet. Every few seconds, I dare look up to see Warren. He has decided to come down the way he came, and the veins in his neck bulge with anger.

Spotting more handholds, I scurry and slide until my feet hit the path, and I break into a run toward the horses.

"*Enough.*" Warren lands next to the horses, blocking my way, mud covering the length of his left side. He must have slipped the remaining feet down the rock face, and his arm looks badly scratched up. His right collarbone juts irregularly, and when he brandishes his knife, his hand shakes. "Get your worthless hide over here or I'll leave your corpse on this mountain."

I stare at him, the man I've spent my whole life fearing. How could I have come from someone so twisted? How could I understand what is right, which way is north, when

I was raised by someone whose moral compass spins out of control?

The answer comes like a fire over crackling logs with both peace and power. *There is more in me than what that man gave me.*

Behind Warren, his horse bites at her bit. Bolo's ears are pinned back against her head as she takes in the sound of the storm, like jungle drums on all sides. Whipping her tail and raising her head, Bolo calls out as though in pain, as though the restraint of staying with her master is more than she can bear.

You and me both, I think.

My bundle of clothes is still on the crook of my arm, though the knot has loosened as I climbed. Grabbing it with one hand, I hold to only the sleeve of the dress that bound it all. With a sudden jerk of my arm, I throw the bundle toward the horse's face. The long dress snaps loudly as I hold one end, the flurry of color invading Bolo's vision.

Bolo throws her head back and bellows, then rather than raising her front legs to run like I had planned, her hind legs become taut.

Warren whirls around to stop his horse from spooking, but rather than flight, the horse's primal instinct screams to fight. Kicking up, both back legs suspend in the air for just a moment. The horse bucks as wild as her ancestors. A hoof catches Warren in the chin full force, snapping his neck back before his knees crumple under him and he falls into the mud.

For a moment, I stare at his body lying there, unmoving.

Bolo continues to act as though the devil himself is riding her, kicking and rearing, slashing the air with her tail as her mane whips around her strained neck. Finally, the fear is more than the horse can bear, and she races into the trees.

To me, all seems still. I look down at the man I know so well, but never understood. His eyes are closed, yet I notice the rise and fall of his torso. He's just unconscious.

How hurt is he? I feel a pull in my chest. Even though he hunted me and would have seen *me* dead, how can I just leave him on this mountainside to die? He had his demons. But he was my father.

Yet . . .

This is my chance to be free.

Running my hand along Lady's sleek back, I know I could be miles away before my father awakes. The rain would wash away my trail, and my disappearing act would be complete. I tilt my head toward the sky, letting the rain wash away the dirt and sweat on my face, and in the distance I can see a blue where it's not raining. As blue as freedom and dreams. The blue I have always chased, always been running after so hard.

Yet my gaze drops from the sky to the mountain trail. The rain has made the colors around me come alive. Looking at the trees, I feel like I've never seen green before. Leaves shake in the rain as though they want to whisper their secrets to me, a gentle chorus of emerald and jade. My thoughts go back to the little warm cabin wrapped tightly in its fields of green. Green as effort and joy, challenge, and most of all, green as love. Green as things that live.

At last, my gaze falls back to my father. He would have killed me. I just had to fight him for my own life. I could leave, and he would only get his due.

But I would always be running, always wondering if he was after me. I want to stop running, to place my hands on my knees and deeply breathe sweet mountain air into my lungs. I want to live in the green.

Resting my hands on Lady, I lift myself onto her back. I look down at my father lying in the mud, nearly as still as stone, and feel something inside me that I don't understand. It balls in my throat and forces a single tear from my eye. Wiping it away with a fingertip, I turn and begin my way back down the mountain trail.

Chapter Fifteen

My finger traces the thread leaves, embroidered so delicately, they look as though they might have landed there on a spring day. I cling to the pillow as if I'm floating in the ocean, and it alone buoys me up. The evening breeze catches the white untouched curtains of an open window, and the doctor's wife comes over and closes it before turning to me.

"Don't worry now." She smooths the front of her dress without meeting my eyes. "He's bound to wake up before too long."

Don't worry? I curl my fingers tighter around the pillow and look at the cream carpet. Worry that he won't wake up, or worry that he will? Right now, I can't feel either one.

There's a rap at the front door, and she sweeps over to it. I don't bother looking up until I hear my name.

"Marian."

Lifting my gaze, I see Henry standing in the doorway. In three steps he's next to me, then sits on the couch and raises his hands to cradle my face. Something inside me

sloshes and tips, like a glass too full. I look into those beautiful brown eyes, feel his thumb caressing my cheek, and it
seems I no longer have the strength to keep myself upright.
I curl into him, and the pillow falls to the ground as my
hands come to his chest. The tears stream, quiet as snow-
fall, down my cheeks. He kisses my forehead, and my cup
overflows.

Each tear relieves the pressure built up inside me, all
that was ugly from the day leaving me. The pain flows out,
leaving only the sweetness of how it feels to have him here,
to be sitting down, to be warm and fed and for once, safe.

His arms wrap around my shoulders with the strength
of a mountain lion, yet his words are gentle as a foul. "It's
over. It's done," he whispers into my ear as he slowly
strokes my hair.

And he's right. All I've dreaded for weeks has
happened. There is no fear of what might come tomorrow,
for today it came. It's a liberation, a quiet comfort, to have
met the horrors I always waited for in wrenching antic-
ipation.

"Wait." I pull back and look in Henry's eyes. "You
should be with Rosalie."

He smiles. "She already woke up. I hope it's okay—I
told her and Jesse everything. How you thought you had to
leave because a dangerous man was following you, and you
didn't want him to hurt us. How you fought him in the
mountains, and then when his horse injured him, you actually came back and fetched the doctor from our house to
help him." His fingers brush back a strand of hair that
caught in my tears. "Rosalie and Jesse both insisted I come
in case the dangerous man woke up. Before I could argue,
Rosalie commanded Jesse to fetch the neighbor to stay
with them, and he jumped up and ran out the door."
Henry, hands cupping my wet cheeks, looks deeply into my

eyes. "You don't have to face your father alone. Not this time."

Leaning in, he closes the distance between us. His lips sweep softly across mine, and my own lips part.

Inside that kiss, the nightmares are kept at bay. I love everything I know about this man, and ache from how little that is. I want to know all his details, want to be a witness to the days and years he spends. To share the same memories, to be able to look back on something beautiful we created from a mess at our feet. I have to believe in this, that the shards of our pasts could actually make a mosaic.

Through the night, a carousel of dreams spins until the dawn's light on my closed eyelids tells the up-and-down of the painted ponies to slow to a stop. Before I even open my eyes, I'm aware of Henry's arm draped across my stomach, of my head burrowed in the crook of his neck.

Opening my eyes, I see the white curtain again blowing in the breeze of an open window. Finally, yesterday's nightmare is over, and I've awakened to a new sun-soaked day.

"Miss?" The doctor's voice sharpens reality, and I turn to see him walking into his living room.

"Yes?" I shake Henry's knee, and he wakes with a quick inhale.

"Your father woke up in the night, but he wished not to be disturbed for a while." He pauses and intentionally meets my eyes. "The horse broke your father's spinal cord. He cannot move his legs. I'd like him to travel to a hospital in Charleston and get their professional help. My belief is that with enough therapy and patience, he may someday be able to walk again." He looks out the window for just a moment, then again at me. "He say he is ready to see you now, if you'd like to go on back."

I nod once, then Henry and I stand together. Yes, I need to see Warren one last time. Today, this ends.

Dr. Allred leads us down a hallway to the corner of his country home where he takes clients. There are two doors, and he motions us toward one while turning to the other.

"I'll give you your time. If you need me, I'll be in my office."

He slips through the door, and for a moment, Henry and I just stand in the hallway. Reaching for the doorknob, I clasp it but don't turn, just staring as if to memorize its details. Something brown swells in my chest, restricting my breathing. My mouth fills with the taste of iron, and I realize I've bitten down hard on the inside of my cheek.

"Mare." Henry shortens my name. My eyes fly up, and our gazes lock. He slowly nods as he speaks. "You can do this."

Consciously, I force myself to stop gnawing on my cheek flesh, then I exhale. Turning the knob, we step into the room where Warren waits.

The man lying on the bed only stares at the window when we enter, and though I know his every feature nearly as well as my own, he seems to me a complete stranger. Though Warren doesn't turn to us, I can see into his eyes, and what I see frightens me as much as his rage ever did. There is a particular sorrow there, as if he is standing on a cliff ledge. His right arm is braced, likely so movement won't aggravate the collarbone I broke. Then my gaze falls to his motionless legs, and it seems almost as if life presented the bill for all the pain he has caused. For all the fire he burned, now there are only stilled ashes. Should I feel happy? I don't. My stomach churns yellow, and my words turn stale in my mouth. For a moment, we are so quiet that I almost think I can hear each other's heartbeats.

Henry's hand takes my own, and he gives it a squeeze.
Okay. I can do this.

"Warren."

He shifts at my voice, but refuses to look at me.

"Sir," Henry speaks up. "Are you aware that your daughter saved your life?"

No response.

"I'm sure you've considered what could have happened to you if you had been left on the mountain."

Warren snorts through his nose, but doesn't take his eyes from the window. "Am I supposed to say thank you?"

"No." I find my voice again. "But you do owe me. A life for a life."

With a blink, Warren turns his head and locks eyes with mine.

Lifting my chin, I meet his gaze.

"You have no more claim on me." My shoulders roll back and my jaw becomes firm, though I wonder if standing next to me, Henry notices how my knees tremble. "You will leave this town. The doctor wants to send you to a hospital in Charleston. You will go, and never return."

He just looks at me for a moment, and I wait for him to spit my words back in my face.

But somewhere in those eyes, I see the gray, the gray we lived so many days in. He's not all black—no one is. I step forward and speak directly to the gray.

"You owe me *everything*. You owe me for your life, but even more for the life you *should* have given me. The one person who should have loved me the most was the one who hurt me the worst."

He swallows, and I think I see his head ever so slightly begin to nod.

"Father." I say the word, and to my surprise, it sits between us wide and calm, a wakeless lake. "This is goodbye."

His jawline tightens, but his eyes turn soft. He nods once. "Okay, then."

That's it.

Turning his head back to the window, it's as if we have already left the room. Henry and I just look at each other, then he jerks his head and motions for the door.

I look at my father and open my mouth, then exhale slowly. Reaching down, I rest a hand on the blanket over his legs. I know he can't feel it, but I hope perhaps something in the touch will be the words I can't say. That they will travel through those motionless legs and up, finding rest in his heart.

Then withdrawing my hand, I turn back to Henry. He gestures for me to leave the room first, and as I walk that brown something that had swelled in my chest seems to deflate, leaving room again to breathe.

"Goodbye."

The word slips at me from behind, and when I turn around, my father is looking right at me. We stare at each other as though we can read the other's mind. For a moment, I feel like perhaps I can.

Maybe it's just my own vain imaginings, but I think perhaps there is something almost like love in his eyes. It doesn't look like I always thought love would. There's no light, no happiness. Instead, it looks like smothered pride and an injured heart, unable to hide behind tired eyes. Yet it's good all the same. It's a look that says sorry in a way words could never do.

But it may just be one more of those beautiful delusions I tell myself.

Then Warren bows his head once, and I'll never know what thoughts spin in his mind.

I nod in response and turn from the room, never to see my father again.

Chapter Sixteen

As I lay under the tree, sunlight reaches through to me, illuminating each new leaf like a piece of stained glass. Branches yawn and stretch their limbs toward Henry's cabin and into the spring sky, their weathered bark clinging to the leaves of palest green.

Two days from now, I will come to live in this green, never to leave again.

Through the cold months, I rode my horse here, the pack of books on my back, and each time they were expecting me. Peeping through warm-lit windows, I would see faces, then as I drew close, the three of them would come to the porch to greet me, the children bundled in a large quilt to keep back the cold. Their arms and quilt would enfold about me like bright wings, then Henry would kiss me in a way that can only be described as home. As he put Lady in the barn, the children and I would begin reading lessons by the light of the hearth, and afterwards, Henry and I would cook dinner together, the children forever underfoot and begging for bites. Then when the children were in bed, we'd find each other's arms and spend the last hours of the day in whispers or sweet silence. It was on such a night that he held my right hand and took my mother's ring off it, then placed it on my left hand.

"Would you marry me forever?" he asked, his dark eyes fixed on my face.

I gaped at the ring, wordless.

"I can get a different ring," he stammered. "Unless it isn't the ring—" He flushed and couldn't meet my eyes.

I laughed, and his muscles relaxed at the sound.

"Yes." The word came out riding the bubble of a laugh. "I will marry you! And it's perfect. There's no other ring I would rather have."

And it *was* perfect.

Like the rings of a tree, my whole history seemed there. The storms withstood, it had seen suffering and struggle, scars, and at last happiness. Through the danger, I'd grown until here I stand high in my mountain home, reaching to the sky yet with some good earth to put down my roots. It's enough to make one feel almost inde-structible.

I hear the cabin door open, and looking up, I see each of them walking toward me, their hands behind their backs. Rising to my elbows, I watch them come with an eyebrow lifted. Rosalie is already giggling, and Jesse darts his narrows eyes at her in a warning to stay quiet.

"Sweetheart," Henry speaks first, grinning. "We have an early wedding gift for you."

They sit on the blanket around me, a slightly awkward act, for their hands are still behind their backs. Once they are all sitting, Jesse mouths, *one, two three!* And on three, they each bring their treasure to their laps.

My lovely old books.

"No," I protest, waving a hand. "They are yours to keep."

Shaking their heads, they look at each other with smiles on their faces.

"The gift isn't the books," Henry speaks for them all. Then, with a sparkle in those deep eyes, he points to his son as Jesse opens his book, *The Call of the Wild*, its dark cover seeming to give the boy courage as his quivering hands steady, and he begins to read.

"'He was beaten, he knew that.'" Jesse's finger carefully follows each difficult word, but he doesn't stumble. Then with a glance at me, I know he's no longer speaking about Buck. "'*But he was not broken.*'" My heart swells to know how much he must have practiced to have read that smoothly. He's not the type to tell someone that he loves them, but in entirely different words, he just did. Reaching over, I run a hand down the child's back, and he smiles in return.

"'For neither good nor evil can last forever.'" Henry's voice comes on the coattails of his son's, this time reading from *Don Quixote* at a paragraph I once underlined years ago, when the words were only a hope. "And so it follows that as evil has lasted a long time, good *must* be now close at hand.'"

His words settle over me, gentle as a blanket of moonlight, and I feel myself nodding as I stare at the small cabin behind them.

"'If I e-e-ver . . .'" Rosalie's sweet voice sounds out the letters we have practiced so many times. Looking at her, I see her eyebrows knit in concentration, her dark curls framing her face, slightly pink with the spring's first touch on the ivory skin she had during winter. She holds a single page of *The Wonderful Wizard of Oz*, which is one of the many that had fallen out and been placed back. Rosalie reads so slowly, so carefully, it's as if each word is a sentence of its own, each carries a weight that can't be missed. "'Go looking for my heart's de-sire again, I won't look any fur-ther than my own backyard.'"

"'Because,'" I whisper with her from memory the words to which I could never relate. Until now. "'If it isn't there, I never really lost it to begin with.'" Our voices stop at the same time, and she beams up at me with a beautiful unrestrained pride, blooming like a lily.

I have to close my eyes to keep from overflowing, yet I sense their oneness even without sight. After so much heartache, just to sit with them within reach, to feel the sunshine and hear them tell me they love me in the best way possible . . . It is enough.

Nodding, I open my eyes. "I can't think of a better gift." I grin, pulling Rosalie onto my lap. Then squeezing my arms around her, firm and soft as love itself, I think maybe it was right to believe in all those beautiful delusions. Maybe they aren't so out of reach as I once thought.

"Alvin helped us find all the best parts!" Rosalie squeals, our faces cheek to cheek.

Suddenly Jesse stands, perhaps fearing the abundance of affection will next flow to him, and he jumps straight up, his arms snatching a branch above our heads. With a swing of his legs, he's in the tree's great arms.

With a giggle, Rosalie jumps up too. "Lift me, Mari!" Getting to my feet, my hands hook under her thin arms, fragile as dove wings, and I raise her into the haven of the leaves.

"Come on!" Jesse calls down as he climbs higher and higher.

Henry looks at me and cocks his head to the side, an impish grin on his face. "Why not? Those britches aren't just good for horseback riding, ya know." Hoisting himself up, he then turns and extends his hand to me, the green leaves and sunshine framing his strong shoulders.

With a laugh, I find a foothold and take his hand. Lifting myself into the green, I look up and see nothing but leaves and sunshine and love. Jesse is highest, his denim legs dangling over a branch.

"You can't get this high, promise that!" he calls down.

"Mari, can you see me?" Rosalie hides her face and body behind a thick branch, though I can easily spot her thin arms and legs clinging to the tree limb.

How I love them. Goodness knows how I love them.

Hand over hand, I climb the organic ladder. A west wind shakes the leaves, making them sound like the pages of a book flipping quickly. At last, the branches become too thin to climb any farther, and we each find a perch. There's a quiet between us as we simply sit in those strong arms and let ourselves be held.

I look up through the last remaining branches to the clear sky above, where green meets blue. It's a sanctuary without walls.

There's no need for them anymore.

And at last I figure out what the trees always knew. I had thought all I wanted was freedom, clear skies leading straight to where dreams come true. But even the bluebirds know when to land. The green world has something to offer that the sky cannot. There is a call from the wild earth that beckons. It tells us, *Here is growth, here life goes on. At times that life may be cruel, even brutal. Yet there is still beauty here to be found.*

Henry reaches over and places a hand on the small of my back. Smiling, I tilt my head to the sunlight and close my eyes, trying to hear what I feel like the earth wants to tell me, what the ancient trees have always understood.

Put down roots, it whispers in the quiet of the leaves shaking, *and learn how to drink in both rain and sunshine in equal measure. For it's* you *that I intend to make the giant.*

Then all you'll have to do is reach out your arms, and I can give you the heavens.

But even more, I can give you a home.

About the Author

Corinne Beenfield loves writing, which considering that you are reading this, makes a lot of sense. She shares her home in the West with her husband, three remarkable kids, over sixty board games, and a collection of books that wants to overtake the house. Since life experience is necessary to properly write, Corinne also enjoys kayaking, hiking, days spent at the lake, being an instructor for The Strengthening Families Program, and traveling anywhere she can find beauty - so everywhere. She writes clean romantic women's literature, and if you want to know when her upcoming books will be released you can follow her on the social media sites below.

 facebook.com/corinne.beenfield.58

 instagram.com/corinne_beenfield

Made in the USA
Monee, IL
10 April 2022

94424660R00079